"I'm Not So Sure That You're Really As Hateful As You Want Everybody To Think You Are,"

Honey whispered. "That's why I parked in front of your house—so we'd have a chance to get acquainted and start off on the right foot."

"Why, you little schemer. You said you didn't fool around—"

"Because I wasn't fooling around. My job was to meet you." She smiled impishly, defiantly. "I'm going to stop you, Mr. Cameron. Your old tricks aren't going to work. I think you're just as scared of all the things that scare everybody else."

"You don't know a damn thing about me."

"I know a lot more than you think." Honey seemed to catch herself. "Everybody's scared, Mr. Cameron. Even . . ." she paused, trembling slightly, perhaps because his powerful body was edging closer ". . . bullies like you."

"Is that what you think I am?" he demanded quietly.

"That's what you just said you were." Her tongue slid out to trace the dry outline of her soft pink mouth. She drew away from him. "We should be natural enemies."

His breath caught. His eyes were fixed on her mouth. "Baby, if you're smart, you'll run."

"I can be foolish sometimes. . . ."

Dear Reader,

It's hard for me to believe that summer is almost over and autumn is right around the corner. For those of us who live where it gets cold, that means we have to start pulling out our sweaters and bundling up our bodies. (If you live where it's warm all year-round, well, we'll just envy you the good weather!) And if you have kids, it's time for them to go off to school, probably providing you with some wonderful quiet time!

During that quiet time I hope you'll pick up more than one of this month's terrific Silhouette Desire romances. We have some special treats in store for you! First, there's the start of a new miniseries from Ann Major called SOMETHING WILD. Its first book, *Wild Honey* is the *Man of the Month*. Next, we have *another* wonderful series, BIG BAD WOLFE, from the talented pen of Joan Hohl. The first book here is *Wolfe Waiting*.

The month is completed with four more romantic, sensuous, compelling love stories. Raye Morgan brings us her unique brand of magic in *Caution: Charm at Work;* Carole Buck heats up the pages with *Sparks;* Anne Marie Winston creates something very wonderful and unusual in *Chance at a Lifetime;* and Caroline Cross makes a sparkling debut with *Dangerous*.

So take time off *for yourself*—you deserve the break—and curl up with a Silhouette Desire!

All the Best,

Lucia Macro
Senior Editor

ANN MAJOR
WILD HONEY

SILHOUETTE *Desire*

Published by Silhouette Books New York

America's Publisher of Contemporary Romance

SILHOUETTE BOOKS
300 East 42nd St., New York, N.Y. 10017

WILD HONEY

Copyright © 1993 by Ann Major

All rights reserved. Except for use in any review, the reproduction
or utilization of this work in whole or in part in any form by any
electronic, mechanical or other means, now known or hereafter
invented, including xerography, photocopying and recording, or in
any information storage or retrieval system, is forbidden without
the permission of the publisher, Silhouette Books, 300 E. 42nd St.,
New York, N.Y. 10017

ISBN: 0-373-05805-5

First Silhouette Books printing September 1993

All the characters in this book have no existence outside the
imagination of the author and have no relation whatsoever to
anyone bearing the same name or names. They are not even
distantly inspired by any individual known or unknown to the
author, and all incidents are pure invention.

® and ™:Trademarks used with authorization. Trademarks
indicated with ® are registered in the United States Patent and
Trademark Office, the Canada Trade Mark Office and in other
countries.

Printed in the U.S.A.

Books by Ann Major

Silhouette Desire

Dream Come True #16
Meant To Be #35
Love Me Again #99
The Wrong Man #151
Golden Man #198
Beyond Love #229
In Every Stranger's Face #301
What This Passion Means #331
*Passion's Child #445
*Destiny's Child #451
*Night Child #457
*Wilderness Child #535
*Scandal's Child #564
*The Goodbye Child #648
A Knight in Tarnished Armor #690
Married to the Enemy #716
†Wild Honey #805

*Children of Destiny series
†Something Wild

Silhouette Special Edition

Brand of Diamonds #83
Dazzle #229
The Fairy Tale Girl #390

Silhouette Romance

Wild Lady #90
A Touch of Fire #150

Silhouette Intimate Moments

Seize the Moment #54

Silhouette Books

Silhouette Christmas Stories 1990
"Santa's Special Miracle"
Silhouette Summer Sizzlers 1992
"The Barefooted Enchantress"

ANN MAJOR

is not only a successful author, she also manages a business and runs a busy household with three children. She lists traveling and playing the piano among her many interests. Her favorite composer, quite naturally, is the romantic Chopin.

Prologue

———

Why is it so hard to say you're sorry? To admit you've been wrong? Hypocrite!

Her desire to return to the fold had nothing to do with unselfish motives.

Honey shivered with dread as she tiptoed gingerly up the pink marble steps. It was a magic spring evening in Pacific Heights, San Francisco's lovely old neighborhood with its magnificent houses hugging their steep hillsides. Far beneath her, past the dark forests of the Presidio, a lavender fog rolled beneath the Golden Gate Bridge.

As always the air was characteristically soft and fragrant with the scent of jasmine. Bright stars were popping out in a darkening indigo sky. The beauty of the night and the neighborhood achieved movie-set perfection, exactly the sort of perfection her father sought to achieve in every aspect of his well-ordered life.

Honey hesitated, feeling uncertain of her welcome and vaguely intimidated as she stood in front of the massive door of her father's mansion.

It was chilly for the first of May, and Honey wished she'd worn more than her flowered light cotton blouse and green shorts. For one thing her father would disapprove. Nor would he like her vinyl boots, nor the wide-brimmed green felt hat that concealed her hair even though the vivid color brought out the green of her eyes. He'd always complained that she was too much like her artistic, bohemian mother and not enough like him, so, to please him today, she hadn't worn the bangles at her ears and wrists she'd wanted to wear. Instead she'd selected gold studs and a single gold bracelet.

She touched the doorbell with trembling fingers, then jumped back when it buzzed loudly.

It was not too late to run.

She glanced down the steps at the tired-looking, battered green car she called the Bomb. The old instincts were still strong. But she had run before, thirteen years ago, to escape her father's deplorable tyranny. Or so she had said. She had married a free-spirited man and lived the nonmaterialistic kind of life that her mother would have applauded.

When her father had disowned her, she had laughed with defiant glee—on the surface.

Well, Mike was dead, and Honey was beginning to realize her life with him had been more rebellion against her father than the life she should have chosen. Coming back to make peace with her father was just one step among many in the painful process of self-discovery.

She rang the bell again.

The door was answered by a small Japanese woman in impeccable white who did not recognize her.

Honey should have known the housekeeper would be someone new.

"I'm Cecilia Rodri—Cecilia Wyatt. Mr. Wyatt's daughter."

The housekeeper's face was politely blank, giving no indication that she was surprised Hunter Wyatt's daughter wasn't slimmer and more beautiful and more elegant. That she wasn't perfect—like him.

"I—I teach school here. . . . Well, not exactly here." *No, not here in this exclusive enclave for the rich and powerful,*

but in a small privately funded school for the disadvan-
taged in one of the city's toughest neighborhoods.

The door widened. "Welcome."

Honey smiled at the irony of that word being used on the threshold of this house where she'd always felt left out.

Honey was ushered past the bold surrealistic mural her mother had painted in the last days of her unhappy marriage into an ornate white room with white couches and white walls and golden-edged mirrors. She remembered that her father did not inspire loyalty in the people nearest him. Help came and went. He had had three wives, her own mother having been the second. Both his children had run away.

The cold, formal drawing room oozed with the unabashed splendor of elegant carved moldings, parquetry and marble, tapestries, antiques and rich brocades. Hanging from the high ceiling in the center of the room was a huge golden cage with a white cockatoo in it.

The room was like a stage set for a grand opera, not a place for real life and real people. For a fleeting instant Honey saw it filled with vibrant warmth and slapdash color as it had been in her early childhood.

Because of the many tall windows and wonderful sunlight, Honey's mother had appalled her father by turning the room with the grandest potential into her studio. Honey remembered the smell of paint and turpentine, the brilliant splash of sensual colors on chaotically stacked canvases. She and her older brother, Raven, had loved watching their mother paint, especially since her studio had been a sanctuary from their overbearing father.

Honey went to the cage and spoke softly to the bird. She lifted her finger and the bird moved closer to nibble at it. The cockatoo was making animated, growling sounds of pleasure when Honey's young stepmother glided down the white marble stairs.

Astella was as beautiful as ever and as golden as the room she had designed. One of San Francisco's most famous socialites, Astella was written about constantly in all the society columns, columns Honey would never have admitted

to anyone that she had the slightest interest in reading, columns she secretly devoured.

Astella wore a white gown of drifting silk and a thick gold
necklace at her throat. She had that rare kind of charisma
that would stand out even in a room filled with the city's
most glamorous people.

"Cecilia, darling. This is . . . a surprise." Astella's husky
voice was cool, unwelcoming. "Do sit down. Make yourself at home."

*Impossible—in this house, with you here and Mother
dead.* Honey looked at the stiff white couches and lingered
near the cage so that Astella was forced to come to her.

The slim, long, scarlet-tipped fingers that touched Honey
to guide her to one of the narrow couches were tense and
cool.

"The room, the house—you've done wonders," Honey
said, feeling like a wayward gypsy surrounded by such frosty
elegance.

"That's all I do," came that cool, faintly exasperated
tone.

"It wasn't always."

"No, but I stay busy." Astella used a scarlet lacquered
nail to flick an invisible speck of dust off the golden tassel
of a white pillow. "As you know your father expects perfection in all things." Her gaze slid from the battered green
brim of Honey's hat down the wrinkled blouse and shorts
to the scuffed vinyl boots.

"Yes," Honey agreed dismally. "That's why he married
you."

"Thank you." Astella said, continuing to look her over.
"You shouldn't hide your hair. Or wear such big flowers."

"I—I know I've put on ten extra pounds . . . since Mike
died. Every day I tell myself I'm starting a diet."

"You should exercise."

"Yes, well, right now it's the end of the school year. It's
hard to find the time."

"You don't *have* to teach."

Honey shifted nervously, defiantly. "Yes, I do."

"Oh, yes. Your precious independence—so you can support Mario and prove to us all that you don't need the Wyatt name or the money. You could send Mario to live with his grandmother."

Honey's mouth tightened rebelliously at the mention of her teen-aged stepson. "She doesn't understand him."

"You're only his stepmother—"

"Astella—"

"We could go shopping together. I could help you choose a more flattering wardrobe."

"That I couldn't possibly afford."

"I could help with that, too."

"No." Honey's gaze traveled to the brilliant greens and reds in the foyer. "I'm glad you left Mother's mural."

"Your mother was a wonderful artist. The mural is famous."

Famous—that was why it had stayed.

Once, Honey's father had said that her mother had preferred her art to him. He hadn't cared for it until she'd made a name for herself.

Astella plucked a white rose from a vase and began to twirl it in one hand.

"Don't you ever get tired of just keeping him happy, running his homes, arranging his parties?" Honey asked.

"Perhaps if I were a talented artist or a devoted teacher..." Astella had begun to shred the rose. "A woman in my position has no need for a career."

"Women with money have all sorts of needs."

"As your mother's daughter, I'm sure you would know." Astella's fingertips froze as a dozen petals fluttered to the white carpet. Then she rang for the housekeeper.

The same old tensions had crept into the room.

After the petals had been gathered and thrown away and Astella and she were alone once more, their conversation resumed.

"I know you don't want me here, Astella."

"Only because of conversations... like this. Only because you always upset your father by being prickly and defensive, by pretending to be such a socially conscious little do-gooder.''

Honey shot out of her couch. "Prickly! Defensive! Me?"

"I shouldn't judge you. I'm sorry."

Honey sat back down.

"Look, Hunter's not himself. He's not up to one of your battles." Astella looked genuinely worried.

"What's wrong?"

"His heart's been acting up again. He's been under a lot of pressure lately."

"So have I, but I can no longer stand it that we live in the same town and we don't even speak to one another on the phone. The only thing I know about my father is what I read in the paper."

"You should have thought of that before."

"I was running for my life. Astella, are you going to let me see him or not?"

"There was never a question of that. He was expecting a call, and I heard the phone ring." She frowned as if something about the call bothered her. "But he should be through by now. I'll go look for him."

As soon as Astella had gone Honey got up and began to pace restlessly, not daring to look at her reflection in the long gilt mirrors because she knew they would magnify the many faults of her bohemian costume as well as those of her figure.

Prickly? Not her! Hadn't she spent her life being kind to others, fighting for the rights of the underprivileged? Defensive? Of course not. She'd outgrown all that—years and years ago!

But deep in her heart she knew that the minute she stepped into this house she became the unhappy, guilt-ridden, rebellious child who'd grown up here; the child who'd never fit in to this glamorous life, the child who'd secretly longed to belong, the child who'd had to prove she could live without it.

Honey moved near the partially opened windows and heard the faint rumble of her father's angry voice coming from the pool area.

She opened a tall glass door and stepped out onto the balcony, hesitant as always about going too near any ledge, even though this one was only a one-story drop.

Her father looked up at her. His handsome, weather-beaten face was as grim and unsmiling as on that long-ago day when they'd quarreled and she'd run away. She lifted her hand and waved down to him.

His frown deepened when he saw her. Her fingers froze in midair as all the light seemed to go out of his eyes. His face contorted. Honey's fragile smile died and she swayed nearer the ledge. The flagstones blurred sickeningly.

In spite of the air rushing into her throat, she couldn't breathe.

She should have realized how hopeless it was—expecting his forgiveness.

Slowly he set the phone on the table and took a single agonized step toward her. Then his hands went to his chest, and he doubled over lifelessly. He staggered, slumping headfirst into the pool. His body, a rigid deadweight, sank instantly.

Dear God! He'd had another heart attack. The very sight of her had killed him.

Honey forgot her terror of heights and bolted down the stairs.

Hunter was lying face down on the bottom of the pool when she reached him. Astella screamed from an upstairs window.

Honey yelled, "Dial 911!" Then she dove into the pool and grabbed her father. She struggled to tow him to the shallow end.

Honey would never remember what happened next. Somehow the housekeeper and Astella were there to help her lift him from the pool. He was so heavy, it took all three of them to turn him over.

When she felt for his pulse there was none. She tilted his chin back and lifted his jaw, opening his mouth, placing her ear there to feel for his breath.

"He's not breathing!"

Honey pinched Hunter's nose shut, opened her mouth, took a deep breath and blew two full breaths deep into his chest. She did this again and again. Then she began to compress his chest, repeating the cycle and praying silently for what seemed an eternity until she heard the siren far below, screaming faintly at first and then louder and louder as it climbed the hills.

After the ambulance arrived, she sank onto the grass, numb and shivering, chilled to the bone, utterly exhausted as she watched the frantic flurry of white-uniformed men fighting to save her father.

Her father's face was ashen. Never once did he move or speak.

Astella brought Honey towels and one of Hunter's white gym suits. "You can change in the bathhouse." When Honey only looked up at her stepmother with dazed, bewildered eyes, Astella pressed her arm. "For God's sake, hurry!"

Like a robot, Honey obeyed.

When she came back, dressed in her father's huge sweat suit with her wet hair wound in a towel, her father was on a stretcher being rushed to the ambulance. She was about to race after him when the cordless phone her father had set down so carefully before his collapse rang.

Honey picked it up as she ran after her father's stretcher.

"Hello." A man's rough, violent voice assaulted her. "I want Wyatt. He hung up on me a few minutes ago. When I called back the first time, the line was busy."

Honey was too drained to feel anger at the caller's rudeness. "I'm sorry. He can't talk now."

"The hell you say! You tell that bastard—"

"That...that *bastard*..." now she did choke on a sob "...that bastard...has had a heart attack or something. Who is this?"

"You tell him it'll take more than a fake heart attack to stop J. K. Cameron."

"No way, Mr. Cameron!"

She was passing the mailbox when she stared wildly around the front of the house for a place to get rid of the phone. She lifted the mailbox lid and defiantly knocked the phone against the metal sides before dropping it inside. Then she rushed after her father's stretcher and climbed into the ambulance.

Dear God! How could anyone, even a stranger, be so callous? Her father's lips were blue now, his face grayer. As she touched his icy cheek, she wondered if he was still alive.

"You'd better sit down and put your belt on, ma'am."

Honey sank against Astella.

As the ambulance sped down the hill, all Honey could think of was that her father was either dead or dying, and she could do nothing to help him. Would he die without ever knowing that despite everything, his imperfect, rebellious daughter had always craved to be the perfect daughter he had wanted?

J. K. Cameron had been utterly forgotten.

All Honey knew was that if her father died she would blame herself forever. She had killed him by favoring her mother even after her mother had died, by never pleasing him, by rebelling against his life-style and his marriage to Astella, by stubbornly marrying the wrong kind of man just to spite him, just to pretend she was morally superior, by never admitting that despite his faults she secretly admired him.

Years after she had married Mike, Honey had learned that her father had suffered his first heart attack the night she had run away.

Yet he had never called her.

Nor had she called him. Not even after the devastation of the earthquake and the almost total destruction of his hotel.

Yes, if he died, it would be her fault.

One
___

Hatred filled Joshua K. Cameron as he shoved past people in the white hospital corridors without bothering to smile or apologize. Not that he was much different today than any other day.

Hatred for one man, Hunter Wyatt, and the need for revenge were the fierce emotions that had fueled Joshua's monumental ambition ever since he'd been a boy of eleven. These sentiments had propelled him out of a tough, impoverished neighborhood, and had governed nearly every aspect of his life—even his meteoric successes.

Only today the hatred was so strong, he almost felt overpowered by it. Suddenly the white walls on either side of him seemed to sag toward him crushingly. He reeled as if he were in an earthquake. Then he realized that the floor was steady. The hospital walls weren't falling. It was the defensive walls in his mind that were crumbling, deluging him with unwanted memories.

He saw a boy screaming as he ran through similar endless white tunnels. He saw that same thin-faced, frightened child clinging helplessly to his mother's skirts, looking up with frozen, bewildered eyes as he watched the big nurse with the contemptuous smile hand his mother his father's pitiful things in plastic bags.

Damn it. Not once had Joshua set foot inside a hospital since those bitter days. He had thought the memories were safely buried, that time and the hardships of his life had dulled the pain. But the memories were like the stabs of an ice pick gouging out his heart and the old agony was as intense as ever.

Beads of perspiration broke out on Joshua's brow and his tanned hand jerked his tie loose. He caught himself. Even though he felt as if he were suffocating, he resisted the impulse to give into his weakness. Instead he took a deep breath and then straightened his designer tie, drawing the knot even tighter before he rushed toward his destination with an even stronger resolve.

He stopped suddenly in front of the intensive-care waiting room. For a long moment he stood in the harsh light, taken aback by the outward perfection of his own reflection in the gleaming steel doors.

Ebony hair, ice blue eyes, hard mouth and jaw—women thought Joshua Cameron movie-star handsome until they found he had no heart, no tenderness. His black suit had been hand tailored in London, the soft, lightweight wool excessively costly. His silk shirt and tie had been bought on Rodeo Drive. The man Joshua saw wore his clothes with such ease there was no way anyone could have guessed that once he'd worn rags, that he'd grown up in the garbage-strewn, gang-infested streets of one of the roughest parts of this city.

Joshua took no pride in what he saw. He hated the man he was now just as much as he hated the boy he'd been, and he didn't pause long to reflect on either of them. He flung the doors open and raced inside like a shark dashing through bloody waters toward wounded prey that would prove a certain kill.

Wyatt was a fool if he thought he could escape Joshua Cameron by fleeing into a hospital bed. Another foe might have let up, but long ago Wyatt had squashed out every drop of compassion in Joshua's soul.

Use or be used. Take or be taken. Destroy or be destroyed. Those were the credos Joshua lived by.

At first glance the waiting room appeared to be empty. Then a shadowy figure at the far end of the room sniffled. A magazine tumbled from a sloppy stack on a low table and a woman bent over and picked it up. Joshua's eyes flicked toward her and then quickly away, his intuitive male radar having informed him the disheveled, slightly plump female was not worthy of even his most casual attention.

Joshua grabbed a paper from the receptionist's vacant desk, scanning it until he found Wyatt's name. Then, ignoring the No Visitors sign, Joshua headed toward the doors that led to the unit and pushed one open.

"Wait! I mean stop! You can't go in there!" came the woman's choked whisper from behind him.

Joshua whirled, incredulous. Who was this nondescript creature who dared tell him no?

"I'm sorry," the creature persisted weakly, her feeble courage seeming to vanish as she shrank more deeply into the shadows.

"Who the hell are you?" He growled, surly now at having been crossed by such a shabby little nobody.

He stalked toward her, his rolling, easy gait the predatory swagger of a street fighter's.

Uneasy, she coughed and sniffed again.

She had a hell of a cold.

"I'm Ho...Cecilia...." she began.

He cut her off. "Do you think I give a damn who you are? I meant do you work here?"

"No. I'm a visitor—like you."

He despised inefficiency and messiness. From the look of her rumpled, ill-fitting, stained white sweat suit, she'd spent the night on that hard vinyl couch, something he would never do. He saw chocolate candy wrappers and grimaced at the thought of her gorging herself on junk food. He couldn't see her hair because it was hidden by a white towel that was messily wrapped around her head like a turban, but he was sure the color of her hair would be as nondescript as the rest of her.

In no way was this plain, no—worse than plain—this slovenly, very forgettable female remotely like himself. He felt like a fool for having allowed her to waste even a second of his valuable time.

She tilted up her sunglasses as if to inspect him as closely as he had so arrogantly inspected her. The defiance in that gesture caught his attention. So, even this dimmest of female bulbs could burn with more wattage than he would have given her credit for.

He leaned down, and she let her sunglasses fall instantly. Because of the shadows and her glasses he couldn't make out the color of her eyes. All he could see was that they were long lashed, that beneath them there were dark smudges, the telltale traces of tears. Her mascara had run down her cheeks as well. He saw the box of tissues on the table beside her and the wadded tissues in the ashtray, the lopsided stack of dog-eared magazines she'd tried to read in the long hours to distract herself.

He decided to leave her to whatever misery afflicted her. He was about to go when suddenly she smiled up at him in a way that was somehow quiet and bravely defiant and surprisingly engaging.

She was a fighter.

Like him.

He felt an odd, tingling warmth. Not pleasure! No way! Why would he feel pleasure that this plain woman was being friendly when he had the phone numbers of dozens of the most beautiful women in California? When he had Simone. He never took the slightest interest in any woman who wasn't rich, famous or beautiful.

But the warm smile continued to draw him, and his own response continued to puzzle him. He raked a hand through his thick black hair.

"You must really be worried about someone," she said softly—somehow extending herself beyond her own problems and sensing his.

He felt in tune with her—which was idiotic. He didn't tune in to people; he used them. Nonplussed, he decided it was way past time to cut her dead and be done with this ridiculous encounter.

"Look." He edged nearer, screwing his black brows together in his most ferocious scowl.

She merely sat up taller, uncowed. "Yes?"

Slice her to ribbons. Now!

Her trusting smile was both brave and defiant.

He faltered. "I mean—"

She kept smiling at him in a way that was somehow so special, that somehow made him sense she was putting up an extraordinary fight to appear brave. She was like a kitten battling a lion.

This was absurd. He balled his hands into fists. She was plain, dumpy even. She was a stranger he hadn't the slightest use for, someone he should rid himself of instantly.

Yet the emotion she aroused in him was mushrooming. It wasn't hate and it wasn't sexual. Nor was it predatory. What he felt was an incredible and bewildering empathy. He sensed a terrible sadness in her, and it expanded inside his chest as if it were his own.

He understood her odd stillness, her uncertainty, her trapped look—too well.

Again he had a vision of that dark-haired little boy of eleven, caged in by white walls, white uniforms. The boy was pulling a man's gold watch out of a plastic bag.

Damn! Joshua closed his eyes to shut out the memory of those small, trembling fingers closing around the cold gold watch. The anger that had propelled Joshua across San Francisco at breakneck speed was gone. Something about her, about this hospital scene had made him touch base with the gentle boy he had once been.

"What's your name?" she asked quietly.

He growled, "Joshua."

What the hell? He never used his first name. Not since he was eleven. He went by J.K. or just Cameron.

He looked at her pale, smudged face. Why was he Joshua to her?

"Where's the receptionist?" he demanded more gruffly, determined to dispel his own incomprehensible mood of sentimentality.

"I'm afraid I sent her in to check on my father," the dumpy young woman said. "She'll be back in a moment." She paused. "You're obviously a busy man. I'm sorry if you have to wait because of me."

"Look, it's okay," he snapped, irritated because he didn't feel irritated enough.

"I've been here a while. I sort of know the ropes. Maybe I can help. Who did you come to see?" she persisted gently.

"Hunter Wyatt." How had he gotten the name out without a trace of the loathing he felt for the man?

Her head jerked toward his, startled. "My father?" Her voice was choked again. And surprised. "You're the first friend to come up. I didn't know he still had any." She cast her eyes down as if ashamed to have admitted that.

Joshua was shocked into speechlessness. She was Hunter Wyatt's daughter!

"Not many, I'm sure," Joshua said coldly.

"You remind me of him."

"I remind you of him?" Joshua's fury rushed back like a tidal wave. He edged menacingly closer, but before he could reach her, his knee hit the low table beside her. He yelped as dozens of magazines and candy wrappers and a book, *Losing Those Last Ten Pounds—Forever* tumbled to the floor.

When he knelt to pick them up, he knocked the box of tissues and a plastic ashtray down, too.

"Hell!"

"Hey, take it easy," she said softly.

He picked up a bunch of magazines and threw them back onto the table.

"He's going to be okay. We have to hang on to that," she said reassuringly.

Joshua avoided looking at her, and she misinterpreted that, too. He felt desperate to escape her, but before he could say or do anything, she took his hand.

Then it was too late, because he felt something extraordinary and totally inexplicable. Her touch didn't arouse the sensual variety of electricity he might have felt for a beautiful woman, but her gentle fingertips were like her smile. They brought a kindly warmth that was infinitely pleasant, that drew him like the heat of a fire when he came in wet from a cold sail on the bay. She had touched him to comfort him—as a friend, and just for a second her quiet warmth dissolved all his cold hate and fierce need to destroy. *It was a nice feeling.*

Her hand was soft and small, treacherously gentle. It seemed to belong in his. He hadn't experienced such a powerful connection to another human being in years. Not since before his father had died.

With a supreme effort of will he blocked those memories. A strange lethargy prevented him from jerking his hand free of hers. The same weakness made him sit down beside her.

She said haltingly, "I'm glad you're here. You seem to understand, and that helps. You remind me of him, you know. I mean the way he was at his best—hard and strong. I used to hate all that. Now I'd give anything if he'd wake up and bite my head off. I've been alone here for hours."

Joshua's hand tightened on hers, his brown fingers threading themselves through hers. *Somehow she was a perfect fit.* "I'm sure it's been difficult," he muttered in an odd, strangled tone.

Though she was tearless, he sensed her profound desolation. Even as Joshua wondered silently what he was doing, he drew her into his arms and comforted her, an action that was as totally out of character for him as his every other response to her had been.

"Yes. It's difficult," she whispered brokenly against his collar, her lips so close, he felt the warmth of her every breath flow through his silk shirt to his skin. "You see, if he dies—I killed him."

"What?"

Her fingers curled into his shoulders more tightly. "It's my fault—the attack. We've been estranged for years. I went home today for the first time in a long while. He was on the phone. He looked up and saw me. It was such a shock, he collapsed. I...tried to save him. I had to drag him out of the pool."

Joshua winced guiltily as he remembered her tortured voice on the phone, his unthinking cruelty to her.

"So that's why you've got a cold and are shivering." He caught the scent of chlorine clinging to the damp towel wound around her hair.

She was blaming herself—for what he had done. His raspy voice was filled with terrible remorse. "Cecilia, it wasn't your fault."

"You don't know! I was a terrible disappointment to him, you see. But he was to me too." She sounded even sadder, as if her childhood memories upset her as deeply as his did. "I'm afraid he never had much time for me when I was a child. There were reasons why I resented him—especially after he divorced my mother. My father remarried. My brother ran away, and I tried to rebel against everything my father believed in."

"All that's in the past."

Cecilia didn't seem to hear him. "My stepmother told me not to come. But do I ever listen? I'm always so sure I'm right. Always trying to pretend I'm the little miracle worker." Her voice cracked. "Who am I kidding? I'm no different than they are."

Joshua smoothed her cheek. He almost touched her lips before he realized what he was doing and pulled his hand away.

"They're talking about putting some little balloons in his arteries or open-heart surgery. Like I said, he's always been so strong and tough. At home we called him the iron man."

"Yeah." His one word was grim.

"Now he could die at any minute. One moment he was yelling on the phone. The next he saw me and passed out. I guess that shows you—underneath the hardest masks, we're all human."

"Not all of us, honey."

She began to tremble, and Joshua clenched his hand over hers more tightly.

"I killed him," she whispered tearfully.

"No, you didn't." Hesitantly Joshua brought his other arm around her shuddering body, discovering she wasn't as overweight as he'd thought. She was just well endowed, and the jogging suit was too big and added bulk.

Her body felt tight and firm and surprisingly small at the waist. She felt good, better than he could have ever imagined her feeling.

He hadn't comforted anyone in years—the women he dated didn't need comfort. Not even his daughter, Heather, and her fierce teenage pain could touch him.

Why did he have the strangest sensation that this woman belonged in his arms? She seemed to think so, too, because she continued to cling as if she would trust her life to him.

Holding her brought a vague softening in his chest that was almost painful. Long ago when he'd waited in the hospital, he'd wanted his mother's arms about him, but she'd been too lost in her own grief to comfort him.

The woman cried soundlessly against his shoulder for a while—until a doctor was paged on the overhead speaker. Then she tensed, listening to it, drawing back, looking up at him wonderingly before she blushed.

"I—I don't know why I said all those things to you," she whispered, feeling awkward suddenly.

"I guess you needed to."

"I'm sorry." Her color deepened. "I know you're his friend, but please don't tell him . . ." She slid further away.

He got up abruptly.

While she straightened her rumpled suit, he watched the way the thick white cotton outlined the curves of her breasts.

When she looked up at him a little breathlessly, her hand pausing beneath her breast, he yanked hard at the knot of his tie. He tore his eyes away on a hot flush. Damn! He was behaving like a raw adolescent.

What the hell was wrong with him? She was Wyatt's daughter. Joshua should hate her for that alone.

But he didn't. Maybe because she didn't seem a thing like her father. Not with her soft heart and sad, plain face and unglamorous costume. She wasn't beautiful or stylish, but she was class—the real thing. Her father was a fake and so was Joshua Cameron.

The unit doors swung open and the receptionist barged into the waiting room. "Miss Wyatt, your mother went out the back way. You can go in and see your father now. He's sound asleep and he won't know you're there."

Strange words.

Honey smiled faintly, profoundly grateful to the nurse. "Thank you."

"Be quick. If the doctor catches you, I could lose my job."

Honey turned back to Joshua. "Thank you, too—for your kindness."

Again Joshua was surprised that her sweetness brought him so much pleasure. He couldn't remember when anyone had thanked him for a simple kindness. Maybe that was because he couldn't remember bestowing many simple kindnesses.

Cecilia Wyatt wouldn't thank him—when she knew the truth.

Joshua took her hand and pressed it. She pressed his back. Even though her fingers were small and soft, they warmed him through.

She broke their handclasp, not he. Then she knelt to pick up her things.

"Sir, can I help you?" The sharp-eyed receptionist was looking him over. "Sir?"

"No." He exhaled a deep breath and straightened his shoulders. "I'll come back later."

"I'll tell Daddy you came by, Joshua."

"Right." Joshua couldn't think of anything to say. He clumsily backed out of the room away from both of them.

Joshua dashed through the corridors as if a dozen demons chased him. He took the stairs because he was too impatient to wait for the elevator, plunging down them two at a time, coming to a sudden stop when a final vision, more horrible than all the others, loomed before him. Joshua fell against the wall and buried his dark head in his hands, struggling to block the memory.

But it didn't matter whether his eyes were open or closed. Either way, he saw a dark, impassioned boy quivering like a coward before Hunter Wyatt's giant-size desk. He remembered Hunter's relaxed, awesome power. He remembered how quickly the boy's hate had degenerated into an awful terror and sickening impotence when he'd yelled desperately up at the man, "If I had a gun I'd shoot you." Joshua heard again the roar of Hunter's laughter, the purr of that hateful voice that had lacerated him with its hard-edged contempt as he ran away.

"You wouldn't have the guts, kid. Because you're as weak and spineless as your failure of a father."

Joshua had made a vow that he would never be weak again, and he had kept it—until today. Until her.

Joshua sat in the bar, hating the golden whiskey because he wanted it so much. Cecilia Wyatt had driven him to this. Funny, how the more he tried to remember her, the more her plain, smudged features became a blur. He could barely remember what she'd looked like. Was she tall or short? What were her eyes like? He didn't know. Her hair?

All he could recall was her grief. All he could feel was his own guilt because he was the cause of her pain.

As once her father had been the cause of his.

Joshua looked up gloomily. What the hell was the matter with him? For years he'd allowed himself to feel nothing except an overwhelming obsession for money and power so that he could use them to get revenge against the enemy he hated. For years he'd moved through life like an unleashed natural force building an empire of his own because he'd always known someday he would use it to destroy Hunter's.

Now suddenly when he could finish Hunter as easily as he could smash the glass before him by throwing it against the wall, Joshua felt only a bleak emptiness and a curious listlessness at the prospect of doing so.

Without hate, who was J. K. Cameron? Without the hate was there even a man?

Hunter deserved to be destroyed.

Why couldn't Joshua do it?

Because Cecilia would believe she had killed her father. Because her anguish took Joshua back to the most dreadful hour in his own life. Because her pain seemed like his own when he'd been a young boy in a hospital waiting room—terrified he'd lose his father.

Because he knew the agony and the hopelessness of the long years of dark, guilty emotion after a death when you blamed yourself for it.

Joshua picked up the glass and brought it to his lips, and only barely resisted the temptation. Furiously he slammed it back down onto the bar, spilling the whiskey. Then he got up and left the bar. The Golden Gate Bridge was backlighted by the red fire of a sinking sun as he hurried blindly down the hill toward the bay where he'd left his car.

Joshua could almost hear the roar of Hunter's gloating laughter. "You wouldn't have the guts, kid. Because you're as weak and spineless as your failure of a father."

Destroy or be destroyed.

A parking ticket was fluttering from beneath his windshield wiper when Joshua reached his sports car.

He grabbed the ticket, shredded it into tiny bits and threw them into the gutter. Savagely he yanked open his door.

He had to finish Hunter off. He had to forget the girl and her absurd power that made him as soft as that ineffectual boy who'd run out of Hunter Wyatt's office to hide.

Joshua had learned long ago that there was nowhere he could hide. Not from himself. Not from the hatred that ate at his soul. Not from this new weakness that had crept inside him.

Hunter was his enemy.

So was she.

Joshua stomped down hard on the accelerator and pulled out into the traffic. Horns blared. Brakes squealed. He heard the crunch of chrome fenders behind him. Shouted curses. A man on the curb was jotting down his license number.

To hell with them all.

Joshua sped into the stream of cars, his mind on Hunter Wyatt and his daughter.

When he destroyed Hunter, he would destroy her, as well.

Two

Was she completely crazy?

Not only had she been disloyal to Mike's memory, but Honey actually felt worried about the hard, bitter man who had stumbled out of the waiting room.

Joshua. She'd upset him as much as he'd upset her. But because he'd helped her through a difficult moment, she hoped he'd be all right.

When he'd stalked so menacingly toward her, his ice blue eyes glaring at her, she'd thought him cold, remorseless even. Then something extraordinary had happened. When she'd looked at him again, she'd seen her own pain mirrored in his beautiful, compassionate eyes. When he'd taken her in his arms, she'd felt an instant bonding with him—the bonding of two souls.

For an infinitesimal moment she'd no longer been the rebellious daughter or the guilty widow determined to grieve forever. He'd no longer been bent on whatever dark goal seemed to consume him.

Now it seemed crazy to think such a thing. Incredible. All Joshua had done was look at her, hold her. He was a friend of her father's. Any man might have offered her such simple kindnesses.

But Joshua was not any man. Somehow she intuitively knew that his actions had been out of character for him.

Honey remembered Mike's sweetly loving nature and felt ashamed that she had been drawn, even for an instant to someone as pitiless as Joshua. Joshua was everything she'd run from when she'd rebelled against her father and his cold, self-serving life-style. Her heart belonged in the grave with Mike.

But there was no denying that Joshua's touch and the warmth in his eyes had woven a magic spell. Just as there was no denying that deep down she wasn't really as noble and altruistic as she'd always pretended she was.

She shook herself. She would have to forget him as Joshua had probably already forgotten her. She didn't want to be drawn to selfish, hard-driven men. He was too glamorous looking. No doubt he had an equally glamorous showpiece wife or girlfriend.

Still, as Honey followed the nurse across the waiting room, she secretly wondered what his last name was. The heart that should have been buried in Mike's grave beat too quickly as a little voice kept asking, "Joshua? Joshua what?"

Hunter Wyatt lay like a sunken doll beneath a labyrinth of twisting tubes, the machines on all sides of him seeming more alive than he. Monitors bleeped. His breathing machine made rhythmical, gurgling, sucking sounds.

Honey pulled back a curtain. High-tech medicine. Why did it have to be so dehumanizing?

Her father's skin was white to gray—the waxen color and parchment texture of death. His tall, athletic frame seemed to have shriveled. The sight of her once vital father looking so terribly ill made Honey feel paralyzed by her guilt and sorrow.

She had lost so many years by being at war with her father—almost her entire lifetime. Now everything that had
divided them seemed so foolish. She took another step toward him and made a silent promise that if he lived, she
would make it up to him. It wouldn't matter that he'd never
said he'd loved her.

Her hand curled over his lifeless fingers and she shut her
eyes and prayed that he would get well, that he would open
his eyes and tell her he hated the way she was dressed, that
he hated the way she never made friends with the right people.

Suddenly she felt his fingers twitch against hers—ever so
slightly. Excitedly she squeezed his hand back.

He stirred restlessly.

With a start she realized that he was conscious, that his
dark lashes were fluttering weakly against his colorless
cheeks. He was looking at her—calmly.

She leaned nearer, still holding his hand. "One of your
friends came by, Daddy. Joshua..."

Hunter's gray eyes focused fixedly on her face. Then they
widened. She thought he hadn't heard her, so she repeated
the name.

His fingers moved wildly. The old unmistakable dislike
flared in his eyes before they rolled back and he began to
sweat and twitch, jerking his hand agitatedly from hers.

Loud beeps erupted from his machines. Chaotic rhythms
danced across his cardiac monitor. His face turned purple.
His body seemed to shrink.

An army of nurses rushed in, followed by Astella. The
technicians pushed Honey aside and began to work frantically.

Her father's eyes closed slowly, perhaps forever.

Astella's cool voice was faintly accusing, "We'd better go.
I don't want to risk his waking up again and finding you still
here."

"No..." A sad smile drifted across Honey's face. She
wondered if her legs had turned to stone as she let her stepmother turn her and push her leaden body out of the room.

Nothing had really changed. Hunter Wyatt had never wanted his daughter.

He still didn't. Not even on his deathbed.

Astella was tracing the chipped edge of the yellow plastic table in the hospital cafeteria with the sharp tip of a glossy red fingernail. Her large diamonds sparkled. Honey sat across from her sipping a diet cola. An unopened chocolate bar lay in front of her beside her book, *Losing Those Last Ten Pounds—Forever.* As always even when they were silent, the atmosphere between them was coldly charged.

Astella's golden hair had an artificial windswept look. Bold silver earrings flashed at her ears. She was too elegant and sleek for the cafeteria, too glamorous for ordinary life, and yet she looked wonderful. Every time she got up, people watched her. The male cashier fawned excessively. She was a trophy, one of the many Honey's father had collected during his long successful life. Honey knew that her own madcap mother, the famous artist, had been a trophy, too.

Honey could barely remember Astella when she'd been a young, immensely ambitious executive in the management of a rival hotel chain. First her father had bought her away from his rival. Then he'd grown jealous of her abilities. On their wedding day, Hunter had fired her.

"Do you want something to eat?" Astella fingered her white leather wallet. The words were kind; her voice was cold.

Honey pushed the diet cola away and twisted her plain gold wedding band round and round and then remembered she should hide it under the table. "No."

"You haven't eaten anything except candy bars since Hunter—"

Defiantly Honey placed her left hand back on the table on top of her book. "I never thanked you for coming to Mike's funeral."

"I came because your father was too busy—as always—to come."

"Yes, as always." Honey pressed her lips tightly together as she remembered the turmoil of that day. "I didn't expect him to. I know how he felt about Mike and our life together. About Mario. We weren't something he could brag about to his friends—"

"Cecilia—"

"You're right. I'm being ... prickly ... defensive. . . . Astella, I'm sorry I came yesterday. I should have waited."

"If you hadn't been there Hunter would have died."

"He saw me. That's why he collapsed."

Astella looked at her with sudden understanding. "No, Cecilia. No matter how I feel about you at times, I—I can't let you believe that. Hunter had taken a call from J. K. Cameron. It was Cameron who upset him, not you. You saved his life. I could never have done what you did. Your father's alive because you came."

Was that true? Honey stared at her in silence, wondering as she remembered the rude man on the phone for the first time. Nervous, Honey began tearing at her paper napkin. "I want to know about Daddy and this Mr. Cameron."

"Hunter's been under a lot of stress. For quite a while. There's a business rival of his, a Joshua K. Cameron, who's determined to ruin him."

"Joshua?" Honey's voice barely came out in a whisper. She felt an alarming spasm of fear in her throat.

"Apparently he was buying your father out—at such a low price that when Hunter pays his creditors, he will have worked his whole life and lose everything. It's almost as if Cameron hates your father personally."

"Who is this ... this Joshua Cameron?"

Astella opened her big purse and dug, finally pulling out a magazine and throwing it onto the table. "There. Read all about him. No doubt he paid someone to get him on the cover. He owns a chain of rival hotels, as well as several casino hotels. He owns an airline, land, and I don't know what else."

"Joshua..." Honey's hands froze. *Why had he been kind to her?*

Honey almost moaned as she picked up the magazine.

His incredible eyes were darker on that glossy cover than she remembered, and his beautiful mouth seemed harder and more insolent. He was standing on the top of a skyscraper he was building, looking arrogant and self-assured as if he thought he owned the world. Honey's gaze flickered—she felt the beginning of a tear—as she devoured each handsome feature.

She had known he was glamorous, too glamorous, for her. He was someone you read about, someone you might secretly dream about.

Her palms began to perspire. Her throat felt tight and dry.

"Cecilia, what's wrong? Do you know him?"

"No. Well, I mean . . . not exactly." Honey's voice was faint, dying away. "He . . . he came to the hospital today."

"He was up to no good."

"He was kind to me."

Astella's beautiful face grew as quiet and still as stone. "You must have misunderstood him. He hates your father—therefore he hates you, because you're Hunter's daughter."

"But why?"

"All I know is that when he was just a boy, he broke into your father's office and told him he wanted to kill him."

"If he hates Daddy so much, why didn't he?"

"What makes a cobra decide to strike or not to strike? I don't know. Your father says he was a coward."

"Why didn't Daddy ever tell me?"

"Your long suit has never been communication with your father."

Honey felt a wave of fresh guilt. Not only had she betrayed Mike by finding this ruthless Cameron monster attractive, she had betrayed her father—again.

Honey flipped through the magazine until she came to the article on Cameron. Astella sat in silence as Honey read, pausing over several paragraphs about the beautiful women in his life. There were several photographs of a beauty named Simone. She was pencil thin, so hatefully skinny that she looked dazzling in her skintight sequin dress.

She looked good in Joshua's arms, too.

"Pretty girlfriend," Astella commented. "His wife was rich. All his women are at least beautiful."

Honey forced herself to read more. Joshua had grown up in the same poor neighborhood where she taught. He'd fought his way out. It seemed he was still fighting.

There was a section on Cameron's magnificent five-story mansion on Telegraph Hill. Photographs were included of his modern art collection. In his spare time he was waging war on his neighbor, Nell Strohm, a longtime Telegraph Hill resident, because she was the owner of the apartment building directly downhill from his house.

Nell was an old friend of Honey's—they'd been sent to the same boarding school. Honey bit her lip and wondered if Nell could be useful. Apparently Cameron wanted to tear down Nell's building because it blocked his view of the bay. He planned to extend his garden. Nell and her tenants were up in arms.

There were several blistering quotes from Nell as well as insolent, sexist-sounding rebuttals from Cameron.

Honey snapped the magazine shut without finishing the article. How could she have found comfort in such a brute's arms? Even in her ignorant state she should have sensed his shallow, debased nature; she should have felt a natural enmity toward him.

Maybe it was that secret side of her, that side that was both attracted and repelled by surface glitz that found him appealing.

He had known who she was. And pretended to comfort her.

Joshua Cameron was a ruthless, selfish bastard, a swaggering ghetto punk who'd acquired money and power so he could bully and ruin others. He would destroy everything he touched—unless someone stopped him.

Dear God. This was beginning to feel like one of her vendettas to right some social wrong. Honey groaned deep in her throat like a frightened animal.

Why me?

Aloud she said, "Astella, we've got to stop him."

"But how? Your father is sick, maybe dying.... Cameron's no fool."

"First, you're going back to work."

"Me? I wouldn't know where to begin. I haven't worked in years."

"You were good."

"Hunter has forbidden me to work."

"Like you said, he's...sick." Honey couldn't say the word dying. "I'd do it myself, but you know the hotel business." Honey sucked in a tight, frightened breath. "I'll work on Mr. Cameron in my own way."

"Hunter will never forgive me."

"Or me."

"You're used to that. You'd probably like to drive a wedge between us."

"Astella, if we don't do something quickly to stop this monster, Daddy will be dead and you'll be out on the street."

"Since when did you ever care about me?"

"I don't want to lose my father."

"You walked out on him thirteen years ago."

"Astella, we're going to have to work together—not against each other—if we're to have even the slimmest chance of success."

"Why do I feel we're doomed?"

Honey couldn't look at her stepmother, for fear she'd give up, too. Instead she let her gaze fall to the glossy photograph of Joshua Cameron. His blue eyes seemed frozen over with some darkly chilling emotion, his handsome, chiseled features unrelentingly cruel.

Honey swallowed. "We've got to stop him, Astella."

* * *

A dozen of Joshua Cameron's top executives and his lawyer, Johnny Midnight, were in his hushed elegant office for a meeting. Cameron was leaning tensely over the model of the grandiose hotel one of his South American corporations was planning to build in Brazil. He felt frustrated as hell about all the delays on the project. Most of his executives were bunched together near the mauve drapes at the windows, staring out at the magnificent views of the city and bay forty stories beneath them, waiting for his next move.

The executives wore dark suits. In his black leather jacket, wild tie and jeans, Johnny Midnight stood out. He didn't look much like a Stanford Law grad, but he was—Phi Beta Kappa and all. His intense black eyes were on his boss.

"Midnight, we've got to get this thing built. We're losing millions per year in interest alone."

"I'm with you, J.K. But what about the Wyatt chain? Their stock took a real dive last night. Do you want me to buy more—"

"Damn it, Midnight, I told you to wait on that. I'm talking about Rio."

"Right." The deep, velvet-edged drawl sounded cool, uninterested.

Yet Joshua knew differently. Midnight's sudden tension was quick and hot like a fever. Even though Joshua was looking at the model, he could feel Midnight's burning black eyes on him.

Midnight could see in the dark. Joshua knew he could damn sure see through him. Joshua's own fists tightened. Midnight already sensed something, but then Midnight knew him like nobody else could ever know him.

"So what do you want, J.K.? Say the word." Midnight shrugged his shoulders and drawled in that casual, gravelly voice that wasn't casual at all.

Joshua looked up at the one man he trusted, his only friend, his right-hand man. Back-street alley or executive boardroom, Midnight could handle himself in a tight spot

anywhere. Joshua and he had fought together on both bat-
tlegrounds.

Joshua was tall, well over six feet, but Midnight was taller,
leaner, swifter—deadlier. In high school he'd been a star
athlete. Joshua's own daughter adored Midnight. Hell, except for his driving, Midnight excelled at everything—business, kids, women.

Then Joshua remembered Lacy. With women Midnight
had had one notable failure.

Midnight's hair was blue black except for a narrow, distinctive streak of white above his right temple. His strong,
handsome face was deeply tanned and extraordinarily alive.

"Say the word, J.K.," Midnight repeated, his voice
deadly and still.

Before Joshua could answer, the phone rang. Ticia's voice
flowed from the speaker phone. "Mr. Cameron, It's Ms.
Cecilia Wyatt again."

Midnight's brows arched. His beautiful mouth seemed
ready to smile, to laugh. Instead he exerted cynical control.

"I know you said not to interrupt you, Mr. Cameron, but
this is the fifteenth time Ms. Wyatt's called. Every time I
hang up, she calls back."

Defiance. The kitten dangled the one string the lion was
tempted to chase.

Joshua felt a wave of powerful, unwanted interest. He
turned away from Midnight so his friend couldn't detect it.
"For all her softness at the hospital yesterday, she's every bit
as bullheaded as her father," he muttered.

Joshua didn't realize he'd spoken aloud until Midnight
chuckled.

"I knew there was a woman. Is Cecilia Wyatt the reason
you don't want me to buy—"

"No, damn it!" Joshua brushed past Midnight and
grabbed the phone. "Ticia, put Ms. Wyatt through." He
covered the mouthpiece. "Midnight, postpone the meeting
till I finish with her."

Midnight nodded swiftly and then ushered the other executives out of the room, returning alone. He picked up a sheaf of legal documents that dealt with the Brazil project.

"Mr. Cameron? Is that you?" Ms. Wyatt asked just a bit too sweetly.

Even with her thick cold, her voice was gentle and soft. Too soft. Joshua didn't like the way it affected him even over the phone. Suddenly he wished he'd told Midnight to leave, too.

"J. K. Cameron," Joshua said coldly, giving her no other greeting. Grim initials and his last name should set the correct tone. He picked up a rubber band and began stretching it with his free hand.

"Thank you for talking to me, Joshua."

Joshua. The sound of his own name raced through him like electricity.

"Get to the point," he growled.

Across the room Midnight sank down into a leather chair, his long legs sprawling. He seemed to be flipping papers with more gusto than was necessary.

"We met yesterday in the hospital waiting room," she said. "You may not remember me—"

What he remembered was the way his skin had crawled with heat when she'd touched him so gently. Joshua didn't like the memory—especially since his neck was getting hot just thinking about it. Especially since he knew Midnight was hanging on every word, on every inflection.

It was maddening the way she always drew out every exchange. Joshua began stretching the rubber band.

"Plump. Rumpled white sweat suit. No makeup. How could I forget?" Joshua demanded cynically. The rubber band he had been stretching popped loose and flew toward Midnight.

"Ouch!" cried Midnight, springing up instantly, rubbing his tanned cheek.

"Sorry." Joshua waved Midnight back down.

"Forgiven," she replied.

"I wasn't apologizing to you," Joshua snapped.

Midnight chuckled as he picked up the legal papers.

"Oh," she said, the one word both defensive and defiant. "I didn't really expect an apology from a man like you."

Defiant. Again. Why the hell did he have to be so drawn to that?

"I didn't realize who you were yesterday," she said.

"I figured that out for myself," he said grimly.

"You must have thought I was a fool—leaning on your shoulder for sympathy."

"No." For some inexplicable reason, in spite of Midnight rustling his papers so maddeningly, Joshua was uncharacteristically gentle with her.

"I'm not sure I want to know why you were there. What I do want to know is why you're trying to destroy my father—"

"Ask him."

"He's in no condition to answer me."

"Ms. Wyatt, I'm a busy man."

"Then I'll make this short and sweet."

"Short will do."

"I want you to back off."

"No."

"Please."

"Please doesn't work with me."

"What will, then?"

"Are you offering to sell your soul to the devil?"

"Something like that." She lowered her voice. "I would do anything to save my father."

"Sorry, not interested." *Liar.* He paused, shaken by his secret admission. "Look, Ms. Wyatt, women . . . beautiful women . . . or at least their bodies are a dime a dozen for a man like me."

"Simone?"

How the hell did she know about Simone? "Damn it! I'm not in the market for souls—if indeed that was what you were offering for sale. As for your body. . ."

He let the last word hang in the air.

A crisp paper flipped noisily on the opposite side of the room.

"You misunderstood me," she said in a low, shocked tone.

"Ms. Wyatt, I've been propositioned before, by women who are far more desirable than you."

Another page of that maddening legal document Midnight was pretending to read crackled.

"I'm sure you have," she said, her voice fainter now.

"Is that an insult...or a compliment?" he countered.

"It was just a fact. It wouldn't kill you to wait, would it?"

"I like doing things fast."

"Why can't you quit buying our stock for ninety days?"

"Why should I? It's at rock bottom right now."

"Because of the rumors you've paid that slick Stanford lawyer of yours, Mr. Midnight, to spread among the right people."

"You're wrong there, Ms. Wyatt."

"My father's sick."

"That's his problem. As soon as I've got enough stock, I'll leak word that I'm buying. Your stock will go through the ceiling. Whatever I do then, I'll make a profit."

"My father will die if you don't ease up."

Joshua felt himself hesitate—inwardly. Why could she bring on this weakness? He forced a coldness into his voice. "Then I'll get control of your hotels even quicker."

"Is that all you care about—business? Doing a deal fast?"

"With your father it's personal."

"You hate him that much?"

Joshua said nothing.

"Yesterday...you seemed like a nice man."

"First impressions..." But Joshua could feel the sweat breaking out on his brow. He didn't like remembering yesterday or the way he'd behaved with her. His fingers itched to claw his tie. But Midnight would see and understand.

"Mr. Cameron, please..."

"Ms. Wyatt, cut the...the niceness. Feminine charm won't work with me. Especially not from a Wyatt."

When her soft voice began to beg, he couldn't bear it. He held the phone away from his ear. Then he slammed it down.

Almost instantly it rang again. Defiance, again. Joshua picked it up before he thought.

"Then I won't be nice," the gentle voice said firmly. "If my father dies, you'll never get his hotels. Because I'll see that you don't."

"Do you really think you can stop me?"

"Oh, yes. I'll do anything to get even with you."

He laughed harshly. "Revenge? I was playing that game when you were still in diapers."

"Are you always so hateful?"

"If I told you, you wouldn't have the fun of figuring me out for yourself."

"You're an arrogant, self-centered, conceited bastard."

"Whatever works."

This time *she* hung up.

Joshua set the phone down slowly, thoughtfully. She was fragile, inexperienced, afraid. A woman like her didn't know the first thing about fighting a man like him. He could crush her easily.

But she was brave and defiant. And nice. Damn it. But she was a kitten toying with a lion. He would smash her anyway.

Midnight got up and strode toward him, his dark face alive, his black gaze more intense than usual.

"What are you looking at?" Joshua's growl was thick, embarrassed.

"Maybe nothing, J.K. Or maybe something that might prove damned interesting."

Once Midnight got an idea in his head, he hung onto it like a dog with a bone. Joshua ignored him and punched a button on his telephone. "Ticia, refuse all calls from Ms. Wyatt."

"Too hot for you to handle, huh?" Midnight taunted softly.

Take or be taken. Destroy or be destroyed.

Joshua glanced angrily away from Midnight. His stubbornness made him a damned good lawyer. At the same time it could make him a damned annoying friend.

"Buy all the Wyatt stock we can afford," Joshua ordered. "And get the hell out of my office."

Midnight just stood where he was and laughed.

Three

Hunter's raspy command erupted from the bed. "Mario's not our kind. You're to send him to his real family, quit that dangerously insane job in that poverty-stricken sewer, and move home. And another thing—stay away from J. K. Cameron, or I'll disown you."

Same lyrics. Same tune. Honey's fingers knotted rebelliously against the curtains of the window as she looked down at the pool where her father had collapsed three weeks earlier. "You already did that—thirteen years ago, Daddy. It didn't work then—"

He pressed his chest as if he were in pain. "So you're going to keep on pretending you're not one of us and refuse to obey me—as always?"

Honey's mouth tightened. "Why change a winning father-daughter relationship at this point?"

The immense bedroom grew tense and silent. Honey left the window and began to pace.

Distaste filled Hunter's eyes as he watched her. "Why don't you ever wear anything that flatters you? Where the hell did you get that awful green hat?"

"A flea market," she said with false cheerfulness. "I thought it was eye-catching."

"Why do you always cover your hair like your mother did?"

"That's why."

"She did it to keep from getting paint in her hair," he said.

"Okay, maybe I'll stop—but, that's not a promise."

"You're stubborn and mean and defiant."

"Who do you think I take after, *Daddy?*"

That was a chilling thought for both of them.

Fortunately before their inane quarrel could escalate, Astella glided into the room. Honey suspected her of eavesdropping.

Glamorous as usual, Astella's golden hair was secured in a tight, gleaming coil at her nape. She was dressed in a white silk business suit.

"You're looking flushed, Cecilia," Astella said coolly as she went to her husband and kissed his brow. "Why don't you open the window and let in some fresh air?" To divert his anger, Astella began to lecture Hunter on medicines and his diet, repeating all the latest complaints of his nurse.

"Mrs. Compton's a battle-ax," Hunter muttered angrily.

"She says even worse things about you, darling."

"I'd fire her except I'll be back at the office too soon to bother."

"Oh, no—"

The conversation had changed abruptly to business.

"You're to stay the hell away from my office, Stell, before you destroy everything I've spent my whole life building."

Astella glanced nervously toward Honey.

Honey exchanged an anxious look with her stepmother before rushing to her. Their alliance was still an uneasy one.

"Astella can't do that because I—I can't fight Mr. Cameron without her."

"Damn it! I told you to leave that bastard alone."

"Believe me, I hate him even more than you do, Daddy."

That was an understatement. These days the mere thought of J. K. Cameron was enough to make Honey's blood heat with fury. "I didn't tell you this, but last Tuesday when I tried to see him he had his guards throw me out of his offices like a common criminal."

"We saw it on TV," Astella admitted quietly. "The mayor was here when they handcuffed you."

"On TV! The mayor!" Honey groaned.

"I think all the mayor could see was the back of your head."

"Then you saw that there were at least a dozen police cars—two dozen cops. You would have thought I'd robbed a bank the way they threw me up against the wall. Why...if that slick Stanford lawyer of his, Mr. Midnight, hadn't come down and said that the handcuffs wouldn't be necessary if I'd promise to quit harassing his boss, the police would have carried me off to jail. Cameron's a monster. A—a—" Honey reddened as she relived the humiliation.

"He's all those things and worse," Astella agreed. "But at least after that initial rather vengeful shopping spree, he's slowed down on buying our stock even though he's manipulated the price so it's at rock bottom."

Astella's cool mind was on business, not passion. She turned back to Hunter. "I'm afraid I've drastically cut our hotel staff."

"Damn it! Neither one of you featherbrains knows what you're doing! Cameron's a spineless wimp like his father. That's why he quit buying. He hasn't got the guts to take on the Wyatt chain."

Honey shivered at the memory of Joshua's ice blue eyes, his hard determined mouth. "I think you're wrong, Daddy."

"*You* think. *I* know. *He's a coward!*"

"Darlings," Astella began briskly, taking a new tack. "We're vulnerable right now. We're overstaffed in management. We need to remodel. We haven't been aggressive enough at promotion. We've lost market share. Our stock's almost worthless. You're sick...."

"I'll be dead if you two keep this up," Hunter roared. "I don't need your help. I don't need either one of you. I never have."

Astella knelt gently, her slim fingers smoothing satin coverlets until Hunter pushed her hands away. He eyed his daughter with equal fury.

"We'll go now, darling," Astella said, "so you can rest." She grabbed Honey by the hand and dragged her toward the door.

"Don't give me that phony darling stuff," he shouted after them.

Close to tears, Astella shut the door. When they reached Honey's car, Astella attacked. "Do you see what you've done? He hates me now."

"Would you prefer that he die? Do you want to risk everything because you're afraid to stand up to him? He's not competent to run his affairs right now. You are."

Astella bit her lip.

Honey adjusted her ugly straw hat, so that its tilt was even more precariously defiant than before. "Look. I'm sorry I always upset him. I made things worse, as usual but, Astella, we can't give up."

"I—I guess you're right."

"You've been wonderful at the hotel. I feel terrible that I haven't done anything," Honey said. "But as soon as school's out, I'll do more."

"Like what?"

"Since he won't talk to me at his office, I'm moving down the hill from Cameron so I can sneak up on him from his blind side."

"Are you crazy? Cameron saw you in the hospital. He knows you. You hate him! You'll attack him the way you do your father and make things worse."

Honey opened the door of her battered green car. Then she turned back to her stepmother. "I've been trying to figure a way around that. I've got to be different than I was that day."

"He's a very dangerous man—a man you dislike."

"Believe me, I know that better than you do. I've got the handcuff bruises to remind me."

Astella was looking at Honey's enormous green hat. "Your father was right about that hat. It doesn't do a thing for you."

"You *were* eavesdropping!"

"If you're going to take on Mr. Cameron, you're going to need a whole new look. You really should let me help you pick out a new wardrobe."

Honey hesitated. She felt like she'd be selling out to make herself look attractive for *him*.

"We're supposed to be working together," Astella said. "You can't catch the shark if you don't bait your hook with something appetizing."

"Shark bait..." Honey shivered as she remembered Joshua's ice-cold predatory eyes, but she managed a brave smile. "I—I'm warning you, Astella. You're not going to like where I shop. And you're not going to like how I have to try on twenty outfits before I find one that makes me look slimmer."

At least half a dozen men looked up from their menus as a fashionably dressed Honey followed a waiter to her table in the posh restaurant. The waiter pulled out the chair by the window. Honey felt uneasy, not herself, like a child playing grown-up in her mother's clothes.

Honey started to sit in the chair, and then she looked down. Fourteen stories down. The sidewalk and rushing pedestrians blurred sickeningly.

Shuddering, she glanced quickly at her waiter. "Could I please sit over there?" she asked pointing to the chair on the opposite side of the table.

"Of course, Madame. Most people prefer the view—"

"I—I'm sure it's lovely."

As Honey turned her head away from the window, the sunlight streamed through the glass and turned her hair to flame. She had cut the remarkable silken stuff into a sleek, shoulder-length pageboy.

A smartly dressed, beautiful young brunette passed her by.

Honey stood up, her green eyes sparkling. "Nell—"

Nell turned. Her brown eyes widened. "Why, Honey. I—I didn't recognize you. Stand up."

For once Honey obeyed, even though she felt more ill at ease than ever.

"You look thinner."

"I'm not," she said defiantly, guiltily. "It's the dark solid color."

"More glamorous, then."

"Astella helped me pick out my clothes. I—I wish they weren't necessary."

"And your hair—! You have the most wonderful hair in the world."

"Astella's hairdresser cut it while she told him how. But... this isn't me."

"Makeup, a new hairdo, a gorgeous green suit that flatters you instead of those awful jeans and bangles." Nell sat down. "Does this metamorphosis mean you've learned the error of your socially conscious ways? That you're finally going to relax and enjoy being the spoiled little rich girl?"

Honey smiled at her friend even more defiantly. "I bought this suit on sale—and I manage on my own."

"Ah— Well, a girl who's too proud to ask Daddy has to be clever. And you always were clever except when it came to men and money—two very important exceptions, love. Speaking of which, what's the occasion? A new man? Could this be love—again? Mike's been dead...what is it...three years?"

"Two." Honey blushed guiltily. "In 'hate' would be more accurate."

"Mmm." Nell smiled. "*He* sounds interesting."

"*He* is. But not in the way you think. He's dangerous."

"He's not like Mike, then?"

Honey flushed. "Hardly. This guy is bad news."

"Great! Mike may have been nice, but I never thought he was right for you. He took himself too seriously."

"His life meant something."

"Maybe, but if he was so great why did you go to pot while you were married to him? If a man is good for you, you improve."

"I—I did improve, but in ways you can't see."

"You're right there," Nell admitted matter-of-factly. "But, I can definitely see an improvement since you met Mr. Wrong."

Honey stared back, her eyes huge and betrayed, completely nonplussed. "Nell, please—"

"Sorry."

There was an awkward silence. Then Nell started talking again.

"Honey, I was thrilled when you called."

"I had a reason. I read that you moved out of your apartment on Telegraph Hill because a certain neighbor keeps running off your managers. Sounds like you need someone to live there and manage your apartment building. I'm volunteering."

"For combat duty?" Nell laughed.

"Exactly."

Nell signaled the waiter. When he came she ordered a very fine wine.

"But, Honey, you teach on the opposite side of town."

"And I've no experience managing apartments. But I've got the summer off. And I'd work very hard. I've checked several books out from the library on apartment management. Tenants can't be any worse to deal with than the kids I teach."

"My tenants are the most demanding eccentrics in all of San Francisco."

"I'm used to difficult people."

"Then you'll probably love them."

"Is that a yes?"

Nell sipped daintily from her wineglass. "It's maybe. And only until I can find someone with experience. And only because I'm desperate."

The waiter reappeared and Nell ordered their meal—lobster with black bean sauce and pine nuts, two stir-fried noodle dishes and a stew of diced chicken in a light cream sauce.

"How's your father?" Nell asked when the waiter had gone.

"A bear. Which means there's room for hope. He's got to cut back on stress. He can't even go near the office for another six weeks."

"At least you're together again."

"Not exactly...and maybe not for long."

"What do you mean?"

"My father has an enemy who's deliberately trying to destroy him. An enemy who won't stop." Honey hesitated. "Nell, unless I do something—fast—I'll be burying my father, and my stepmother will be penniless."

"Good Lord! Who is this man?"

Honey pulled the magazine with the article about Joshua out of her purse. "Your famous neighbor."

"J. K. Cameron? The same disgusting jerk who's determined to buy my building and tear it down? Honey, no..."

"Nell, I despise the man, but I *have* to get acquainted with him...on a personal basis."

"Are we talking seduction?"

"Are you out of your mind?"

"Then what? Why the hair? The new you?"

"He saw me in the hospital a month ago. I—I couldn't take a chance that he might remember me. Fortunately I looked terrible that day. No makeup, or rather what makeup I did have was running all over my face. I had sunglasses on. My hair was wet and wrapped in a towel. I was wearing one of Daddy's old jogging suits."

"Honey, forget it. J.K.'s sharper than you think."

"Nell, we grew up together and you walked right past me."

"Well . . ." Nell studied her friend and silently conceded that point. "Even if he doesn't figure out who you are, even if he was the kind of guy you could befriend, you'd be crazy to pick my building. He absolutely loathes it and everyone who lives in it. He made me the most abysmal offer for it. Not that I want to sell to him at any price. Some of my tenants are dear, old things who've lived there for years. If he buys, he'll kick them all out."

"What's he like?"

"If you know enough to despise him—?"

"I mean . . . details."

"Oh, he's just great if you like utterly ruthless, ice-hearted, egotistical, womanizing barracudas."

"I was raised by one."

"Honey, he'd sleep with you in a second, and still finish your father off without a qualm. Quite a change from your sensitive, socially conscious Mike."

"Yes." Honey clenched her napkin. "I've tried calling Mr. Cameron, but he won't talk to me any more. I don't have an entrée to the crowd he socializes with, so I can't get to know him that way. Nell, you're my only chance."

"He'll eat you for lunch, darling and then nibble on some other beauty for dinner. He's got a daughter, but he shipped her off to boarding school when his wife left him."

Honey shivered. "Nell, please give me the job."

"You're going to be miserable there. The apartment is post-earthquake—1906, that is. People kill for a parking place up there. You'll have to pay someone to haul your garbage up the Filbert Steps. My tenants are a real hassle. Mario and his friends and his drums won't fit in there."

"If I promise no drums, will you hire me?"

Nell nodded slowly, dubiously.

"Thank you. You won't regret this."

"I'm not so sure. But as I told you, I'm desperate."

With renewed fear, Honey remembered Joshua's black-lashed icy blue eyes, his cruelly sensual mouth, his chillingly harsh voice over the phone. But the most terrifying memory of all was that of her own vulnerability when he'd gently held her in his arms at the hospital.

Honey sat frozen across the table. "Oh, Nell, I'm desperate, too."

Four

Honey had awakened that morning with a sick stomach and a fluttery heart. Now she had the beginnings of what felt like a migraine. Today was the day she was moving into Nell's apartment.

The Bomb seemed to be as reluctant as she to make the final climb up Telegraph Hill. When Honey pressed hard on the gas, the engine wheezed. Something under the hood popped.

Honey stomped harder. Her car made a final gasp and rolled backward.

The taxi driver behind her honked frantically, and she braked just as the Bomb's bumper nudged his.

Union Street was so steep, it would have been hard for the Bomb to climb it any day, but this afternoon the struggle was even worse than usual because she had loaded it to the brim with schoolbooks, boxes of papers to grade, Mario's broken guitar and her kitchen appliances. Not to mention her cat, Mr. Right.

She turned her key in the ignition. The Bomb started, only to die and roll backward when she put it in gear and touched the gas pedal. The taxi driver kept honking furiously. She twisted her key again and stepped on the gas, flooding the engine. Again she tried, only for her car to sputter to life and die the second she took it out of neutral.

She threw up her hands, gesturing helplessly at the cabbie, but instead of getting out to help her, he swerved past her, screaming in Italian, shaking an angry fist over his roof. Mr. Right began to meow anxiously from his cat carrier on the floorboard.

Dear God. Starting the car once more, she revved the motor, determined to warm it up before she tried to climb the hill again. She nibbled on a chocolate candy bar—forbidden stuff now and, therefore, all the more delicious—while she raced her engine and wished she'd waited till next weekend to move in, when school was finally over and she felt braver. After three full minutes in neutral, she threw her empty candy wrapper onto the floorboard, put the transmission in first and inched up the hill, fluttering her toe against the gas pedal the whole way.

She turned onto Montgomery Street. At the bottom of the slight hill beneath the trees that hid Coit Tower, she saw Joshua's five-story ultramodern pink mansion hugging the right side of the hill beneath her. Beyond them both the blue bay glittered.

Of all the damnable good luck! Usually the narrow, tree-lined street was jammed with cars. Why couldn't it be today? What was that roomy parking space doing directly in front of the Filbert Steps right where she was going?

She drove past it and parked in the illegal space in front of Joshua's house, deliberately blocking the entrance to his garage. Tilting her sunglasses up, she twisted her rearview mirror and defiantly fluffed her bright bangs. That quick glance told her that there was no way Joshua would ever associate the pretty, albeit chaotic-looking creature in the mirror with the grief-stricken wreck he'd met in the hospital waiting room a month earlier.

Hurriedly she got out of her car, first making sure Joshua's windows were dark and that he wasn't watching before she opened her hood. Her guilty gaze flicked to the distributor cap and then away, her frightened heart thumping. She couldn't resist a second wary glance up at Joshua's closed miniblinds. Then, fast as a rattler striking, her hand darted inside and yanked the emission-coil wire loose. She closed the hood, scanned the darkened windows again and began whistling softly, innocently as she pretended to watch two puffy clouds sail over her head.

The battle lines were clearly drawn now. She couldn't be the little coward she wanted to be.

She dusted off her hands and then dug for a scrap of paper in her purse. Licking the tip of the pen for inspiration, she leaned over her hood and wrote furiously, her breezy note telling Joshua where she would be in case he needed in or out of his house. When she was done, she tucked the paper under a windshield blade.

Mr. Right meowed, perhaps appreciatively, as she lifted his cat cage out of the Bomb along with a box of bedding. Telegraph Hill was so steep that Filbert Street, which crossed Montgomery, became nothing more than a charming easement which was used for a garden by the residents. Narrow wooden steps provided pedestrians access to their homes on the hill and to the streets below. Because Nell's building fronted on the steps and the garden, Mr. Right would be able to be both an indoor and an outdoor cat for the first time in his life with no danger of being run over by a car.

As Honey descended the famous Filbert Steps, she walked nervously past Joshua's front door. Picking her way carefully in her high-heeled green sandals as she walked to her new apartment, she saw another cat prowling through the ivy investigating bees and plump roses. Mr. Right meowed again, and Honey smiled. Even if their new apartment was too near Joshua's house for her own comfort, at least her cat would have a perfect environment.

Before entering Nell's building, Honey looked up again at Joshua's house. He was right. Nell's building did block part of his view of the bay.

Once inside her living room, she forgot Joshua and opened Mr. Right's cage, smiling when he slunk out to investigate. The three rooms of the one-bedroom apartment were large and airy. As she followed Mr. Right through them, she imagined the walls white and the trim apple green—to match her curtains and furniture.

She took out a dust rag, but when she ran the cloth over a windowsill, loose paint flicked to the worn carpet. She left off dusting and decided to make her bed.

The apartment was half the size of the one she and Mario had been living in. Mario was going to have to sleep on the living-room couch. As she draped a fresh sheet over her bed, she wondered how they would get along in such a tiny space. Where would he practice his guitar? Where would he entertain his buddies? Where would he park his motorcycle? Could he survive three whole months without his drums?

Honey went to the window. The sun had vanished below the roofline of Joshua's mansion, and his house cast its long shadow over hers.

Her hands shook as she remembered his words. *Are you offering to sell your soul to the devil?* He had spoken then, not of women's souls, but of their bodies being cheap commodities to a man like him.

She remembered how safe she'd felt in his strong arms, how she'd felt an instant treacherous bonding between them. He'd reversed himself and been coldly insolent over the phone and brutal when he'd ordered her arrested outside his offices.

Who was Joshua Cameron, this man who could be both kind and cruel to the daughter of a man he hated? She was afraid as she'd never been before, but it was too late to turn back.

Challenging Joshua Cameron on his own turf would be like diving into the deepest, coldest waters of San Francisco Bay and deliberately seeking out a man-eating shark.

Dear God. She dreaded tangling with him again. She had enough problems already, and all of them would be made worse by living here. Just trying to park would be a nightmare. Enduring Mario's lip-curling complaints when he found out he would have no privacy, listening to him practice—not to mention moving everything they both owned—would make her life far from comfortable.

But worst of all there would be Joshua.

The long, slanting shadow of Joshua's house blocked out all light.

Suddenly it all seemed like too much.

But she had no choice. Her father's life was at stake.

Joshua's right temple throbbed painfully as it always did when he talked to Heather and she complained about the posh, overpriced school she was damn lucky to attend. Only this was worse.

Joshua leaned against the stark white wall on the third floor of his home and wished he'd let his machine answer the phone.

"You're not listening. Daddy, I've been expelled!"

"Young lady, I want to talk to Mrs. Stanton."

"It won't do any good. Even if you bribe her again with some huge donation, I'm not staying at this snotty place one more day. The kids all hate me, and I hate them. They're spoiled rotten—"

Joshua's vision clouded with red as he remembered the bleak, graffiti-spattered walls of the dangerous schools he'd been forced to attend as a child. "Spoiled! Look who's talking."

"Just come get me," she commanded as imperiously as he might issue orders to his underlings.

"Heather, I've got an important appointment at six."

"Am I ever important, Daddy?"

Through gritted teeth he replied. "Of course you are... sweetheart."

The line went dead, cutting his clumsy endearment in half.

She had hung up on him.

Teenagers! If only they could be bottled with a tight cork and locked in a vat like fine wine until they matured.

Joshua slammed the phone down. Then he raced past the dozens of fabulous paintings that decorated his stairwell, down the graceful, five-story spiraling staircase that had cost him more than most men spent on their entire homes.

He set his burglar alarm. Then he opened the door that led to his garage, groped through the darkness and got into his low-slung sports car. He took a deep breath, but the rich smell of leather in no way soothed his taut nerves. He wished he was good with kids—the way Midnight was. Joshua was almost afraid to pick up Heather in his present mood. He'd be too harsh.

With one hand he punched the automatic garage-door opener. With the other he dialed Midnight on his cellular phone.

"Midnight, Heather's been expelled from the Stanton Academy for Girls. You've got to pick her up from her school."

"What about the Brazil meeting?"

"I'll have to handle it without you. You're better with Heather than I am."

"You're her father, J.K."

Joshua exhaled bitterly. "And not too talented at the job."

"Heather's the one thing I envy you, J.K."

"Good. Then you won't mind picking her up for me."

"I'll look forward to it."

"I know I should do it myself—"

"Maybe after we wrap this Brazil deal you could take her somewhere special, just the two of you. Let her pick the place."

"Thanks, Midnight. I'll owe you."

"That's mutual."

"And Midnight—keep to the speed limit as long as you have Heather in the car."

Joshua pressed a button and broke the connection. They never bothered with goodbyes.

The garage doors rose slowly. Brilliant sunlight streamed inside.

He was about to start his car when he saw *it* parked in *his* driveway.

Whatever *it* was, *it* was immense and painted an awful shade of the most piercing psychedelic green.

His black head jerked around. What the hell—

His blue eyes froze on dented green steel. Some sort of horrible jalopy, some weirdo's junkyard creation, was jammed at a crazy cockeyed angle across his drive. It had a Chevy body and a Buick grill. A green note fluttered saucily from a windshield wiper.

He felt like ramming the heap. Hell, the thing was probably built like a Sherman tank.

Joshua got out of his own car and tore the note from beneath the blade, his hard gaze swiftly skimming the jaunty handwriting. Just as swiftly, he crumpled it up.

He unwadded the paper slowly. His gaze narrowed on the swirl of black ink as he reread the name and apartment number.

Honey Rodriguez. Who the hell was she?

From the address he figured out that she was Nell's new manager.

Which meant she was J. K. Cameron's new adversary.

He peered inside the filthy windows and saw that her garish wreck was piled to the roof with old boxes. She was obviously moving in.

Into *his* neighborhood.

Joshua smiled grimly at the prospect of meeting her. Maybe if he was very ugly to her today, he could run her off before she got settled. He felt like being ugly. Maybe it would help him get his mind off his impossible relationship with Heather.

As he strode forcefully toward the Filbert Steps, he heard a soft, unhurried voice singing a currently popular love song.

Some people had nothing to do.

He stopped at the top step. Beneath him, a voluptuous young woman in tight green shorts and spiked green heels was singing to herself as she climbed up the wooden steps, as if she had nothing else to do but to enjoy her life.

He looked at her closely. The instant he did some feeling that was rich and hot let go inside him and seemed to flood his veins. He felt he knew her, that he'd shared some important intimacy with her.

He'd never seen this indolent, harum-scarum creature before.

Not in this life.

And he didn't believe in any other.

Five

Joshua stared at the whimsical, gypsylike creature in green.

Then it struck him. She had a thing for green.

Green car. Green note. Green shorts. Green heels.

She was Honey Rodriguez. He knew it in his gut. Suddenly he forgot the packaging and viewed the contents with a mixture of surprise and pleasure.

Golden-toned ankles and lushly curved calves. Voluptuous thighs.

She wasn't skinny—the way he liked *his* women.

But she wasn't bad.

Joshua tightened with hot excitement. Which was ridiculous. His mission was to destroy her before she even moved in. Besides he liked sleek glamour, women who made other men envy him.

She stopped singing and knelt for a moment to touch a lush green fern and then to smell a fat yellow rose, her every movement charmingly sensual and lethargic. A hummingbird buzzed by her nose and she laughed.

How could this chaotic creature block his driveway and then waste time in the garden?

Her red hair caught the sunlight and seemed to gleam with a fire all its own. He had never seen hair quite that remarkable dazzling color. It was a dozen different shades of red, and all of them were ablaze.

She kept her glorious head down, even when she resumed climbing and singing, so he couldn't see her face. He wondered if she was deliberately keeping it hidden from him.

She was wearing green walking shorts and a long-sleeved, green, cotton shirt. Huge bangle earrings danced at her ears. She was big at the top and a shade hippy, but her waist was small. And somehow on her, her hips and legs were gorgeous.

"Excuse me," he growled with calculated fierceness. "Are you Honey? Nell's new manager?"

She jumped back, choking in the middle of a word. She looked up at him slowly, warily. Then her infectious smile lit her face and brightened something inside him, too. Again he felt the oddest sense of familiarity.

He had to tell himself that the face that was tilted up to his wasn't beautiful. It was merely animated and eager to please. And yet she seemed beautiful, in some special way all her own.

The softness of her mouth and skin registered, too. She licked her lips nervously, and he felt a sudden stirring in his loins.

She climbed nearer, and he realized anew how voluptuous she was.

Too voluptuous. He didn't like lushly feminine women.

"I asked you a question!" he repeated.

"Honey—that's me," she said softly in a slightly trembly voice, as if she were afraid and yet determined not to appear so.

But he liked soft.

She drew a nervous breath and fluffed her glorious hair. He watched the ripples of fire playing through the satiny

softness as it cascaded in waves against her creamy cheeks
and throat.

It was now an effort to force anger into his low tone.
"Then this is your...er...car, I presume?"

"You mean the Bomb?" Again the faint tremble in her
voice.

At least the vehicle was appropriately named.

"Did you know you're illegally parked?"

"Oh, my— Yes." She didn't look at him. "Didn't you get
my note?"

Now she tilted her sunglasses up and looked at him quiz-
zically, and for that brief brave moment there seemed
something oddly familiar about that pert gesture. *Damn it.
He was sure he'd seen her somewhere.* She put her glasses
back down quickly. But not before he had seen her eyes.

He would have remembered her eyes if he'd ever seen
them before. They were as startlingly lovely as her remarkable hair. They were vividly green, long lashed and won-
derfully slanted. But their bright spark had quivered as if
with fear when she'd looked at him.

Why did he imagine her in his bed, afraid of him no
longer, her legs wrapped around him, her fiery hair brush-
ing his chest, those green eyes darkening with desire, her
arms and lips passionately clinging?

Hesitantly she joined him on the top step. She stood close,
too close for either of them to feel comfortable. It was be-
coming an effort to remind himself that he liked sophisti-
cation and experience as well as glamour in his women, an
effort to remember that he couldn't possibly be attracted to
some naive, offbeat creature who seemed to be stepping out
of a sixties' time warp.

Ms. Rodriguez wasn't his type. Not at all.

Why then did he see himself reflected in her sunglasses as
if he were a man spellbound?

"I'm sorry if I'm blocking you," she said in a defiant
voice that made him wonder if she really was.

He was aware of the elusively provocative scent of jasmine. Again he told himself that he had always preferred slim, glamorous, sophisticated beauties.

Glamorous and sophisticated *she* wasn't.

Alluring in her own special way *she* was.

She scared the hell out of him.

"It'll just take me a sec to start my car. Then I'll be gone." Her smile quivered as she tilted her sunglasses up once more, dazzling him again with the innocent heat of those frightened green eyes.

For some reason her smile unnerved him and put him off balance. Again it seemed vaguely familiar. Which was ridiculous. He couldn't have forgotten those eyes. That hair. Those legs. Her smell.

He couldn't have forgotten her.

"It's nice to meet you, Mr. . . . ?"

"Cameron." Even though he gritted his teeth, his growl was lower, less angry.

"I always like to know my neighbors."

"I usually try to avoid knowing mine."

"Usually?" She laughed then, as if she were forcing herself to relax, and held out her hand which was soft and small.

The closer her hand came to his, the more it trembled.

Rudely he ignored her hand even though he felt drawn to take it. Because of her fear he found it impossible to be as ugly to her as he had originally intended to be.

He would size her up. He could save the ugliness for later when he knew more about her vulnerabilities.

"Nell warned me about you," she said.

Why the hell was that such an unpleasant surprise? "Start your car," he said grumpily, determined to end this encounter as soon as possible.

"Aye. Aye." She saluted him mischievously and tripped jauntily toward her car.

Never had big hips seemed so deliciously feminine as they swayed in those tight, boyish shorts. He couldn't help a slow grin of aesthetic appreciation.

No way could he have ever forgotten that walk. And yet that vague sense of familiarity lingered in the back of his mind. *He had definitely seen her somewhere before.*

She turned, her long hair flaring flirtatiously like a coppery fan before it fell back against her neck and shoulders. She smiled. "Coming?"

She seemed to be growing more self-confident by the moment. She didn't wait for his answer, but hopped into her car. When she tried to start it, the engine turned over but didn't catch.

That figured. He raced after her. She was still trying to start it when he yanked her door open. "You're going to run the battery down doing that," he muttered.

"Would you like to try?" she asked, scooting over. Not that she could scoot far, since her front seat was jammed with boxes.

When he got in, his hand accidentally brushed hers. Light fingertips, satiny and warm, skimmed against his. Joshua felt an uneasy prickle of male interest and was gratified when she quickly jumped away from him.

She would be an easy conquest for a man of his experience and sophisticated expertise. *Not that he was interested.*

"You have to put your foot on the gas. Gently. Like this," he whispered authoritatively.

"Oh." Her big green eyes watched him. "My!"

He pressed the gas pedal while he turned the key. The engine cranked endlessly just as it had for her.

Which infuriated the hell out of him. "Something's wrong," he growled.

"I know."

He pressed the hood release and got out, grabbing the loose emission-coil wire the instant he saw it. "Have you been fooling around under here?"

Her eyes were wide, almost fearful again. "Who me?"

Ridiculous question. A woman like her wouldn't know the first thing about cars. As he leaned over and reattached the wire, she got out and began removing boxes from the other side of her car.

"It should start now," he said a short while later, slamming her hood closed.

"You already fixed it?"

He liked the way she sounded impressed as she set her box on the sidewalk. "A wire was loose."

"Thanks a lot." She picked up another larger box and turned toward the wooden stairs that led down to her apartment.

"Hey!" he yelled, freshly irritated. "What the hell do you think you're doing now? I started this thing, so you could move it out of my way. Put that damned box down. I've got a meeting."

When she stepped backward, her green heel caught on the curb. The heavy box she was holding caused her to lose her balance and she tumbled back, dropping the box. Its contents spilled, rolling downhill toward him.

Before he could jump aside, a runaway paint can with a bit of green lace tangled around the wire handle slammed into his shin.

"Ouch!" He danced on his good leg.

She got up slowly. He doubled over to wrench his pant leg loose from the can. Expensive wool fabric tore.

"Oh, I'm sorry." Unhurt from her fall, she rushed toward him.

He didn't look up from the hole in his slacks or the paint can. "Are you always this clumsy?"

She bent down beside him. "Always—when someone screams at me."

Her gentle, frightened voice brought an unpleasant emotion that he was not accustomed to—guilt. But before he could react to it, she touched him. Her fingers pushed his trouser leg up and her fingers slid against his bare leg to inspect his injury.

Her nearness and that light caress of fingertips made it impossible for him to control his breath and chaotic pulse.

He grabbed her hand. "Hey, I'm okay," he said roughly.

"I'm glad you're okay. I—I'll buy you a new suit...."

"There's no way you could afford to."

"I—"

"Forget it!" he snapped.

He picked up her paint can and untwisted the bit of green lace. He was embarrassed when he saw that it was composed of two cups held together by green satin straps—her bra. As he stood up with the flimsy strips of lace dangling from his brown fingers, funny little darts of feeling flooded his stomach.

First she took the paint can from him. Then with eyes and cheeks as bright as his, her bra. But not before he had imagined full, soft breasts, their pouting dark nipples cupped pertly by green lace. Not before his heart had begun to pound with fresh violence.

"I'm afraid I can't resist green," she said, her eyes full of humor and mischief now instead of fear.

Apparently neither could he. Because even though he was late for his meeting, he helped her gather her things. When she began to reload her box in a haphazard, lazy fashion, he couldn't resist lending a little of his male expertise.

Sinking back on those voluptuous haunches, she watched him pack the box with amazed pleasure and gratitude. When she handed him a last bundle of towels, their hands brushed again. This time she didn't pull her hand away quite as quickly.

Tell her to move her car so you can go. Run her off.

"I'll carry this down for you," Joshua heard himself say in a low, gravelly tone he scarcely recognized as his own. "It's the least I can do after causing you to fall and spill everything."

Fool! What the hell are you doing—helping Nell's new manager to move in?

When they reached the door of Honey's apartment, she slid through the opening with him.

"Where does this go?" he asked her, suddenly more aware of her than ever in the small, closed apartment.

"Just set it down in my bedroom," she said, her voice light and breathy. "Here—I'll lead the way."

It was impossible for him to ignore her sexy walk. He was openly grinning when they reached her bedroom. He glanced around. "Where now?"

"On my bed."

He tensed. "Right."

The green bedspread was the same color as her bra. A huge gray cat with a green rhinestone collar lay in the center of the bed.

"Green collar, I see."

"I told you my weakness . . . for green."

Her eyes were wide and inquiring and no longer fearful. Did she sense she had somehow acquired the upper hand? Her mouth was moist—delicious looking.

"One of many—" The words rasped over his suddenly dry vocal cords.

"Yes, I'm afraid so. I'm very messy, very disorganized. I have a weakness for chocolate and for bubble baths on lazy Sunday afternoons—"

"I like chocolate, too." His eyes were on her face. "You're very lovely."

She recoiled warily and glanced away.

Slow down, J.K.

When the mattress dipped under the weight of the box Joshua set down, the cat meowed, stretching a lazy paw indignantly.

Joshua hated cats. "We've disturbed someone's nap," he said, pretending an interest in her pet.

"Meet Mr. Right," she said more easily, now that their subject was safer.

Mr. Right and Joshua stared at one another. Mr. Right flattened his ears.

"He looks like a stray."

"I collect strays." She paused. "They make the best pets." Her eyes touched Joshua's. "Thank you for carrying that down. I didn't expect you to." She paused.

"You're...not at all what I thought you'd be like. I mean—" She edged away.

Suddenly he was thinking of the green bra and the green bed, as well as the fact that he was very much alone with her in her bedroom. He imagined her lying on that bed, stretching her hands up to him invitingly.

She must have read his mind because she moved even further from him, out of the bedroom and through the front door. She stepped onto the porch, folding her arms across her chest, heaving a nervous sigh. He followed her outside, glad to be out of the apartment.

He said in a matter-of-fact voice, "Nell's old manager lived here, too."

"I'll just be the summer manager," she said a little defiantly.

As always, defiance compelled him. "Don't get too comfortable. You won't make it through the summer here."

Her green gaze dared him. "Says who?"

"I'm going to buy this firetrap and tear it down."

"What about the people who live here?"

"They're not my concern," he said. But he had turned away to avoid her quick look.

"No. They're mine," she challenged softly from behind him.

He whirled, edging closer, cornering her when she tried to run past him off the porch. The scowl on his dark face was not nice. "Don't even think about taking me on. I crush people who try to stop me."

Fear flared just for a second in her eyes, and then that damnable, charming defiance was back. She forced a smile. "How do people defend themselves against people like you?"

"They don't."

Although she said nothing, her eyes sparked.

He eyed her just as grimly. "I'm glad that's settled."

"Did it ever occur to you that I might motivate you to change your mind?"

Joshua towered nearer. "What do you mean?"

"I mean," she whispered, "that I'm not so sure that you're really as hateful as you want everybody to think you are. Oh, I know that you've harassed all Nell's managers into quitting."

"What?"

"That's why I parked in front of your house—so we'd have a chance to get acquainted and start off on the right foot. I'm afraid I even pulled those wires under my hood loose."

"You what?"

She smiled impishly, defiantly.

"Why, you little schemer. You said you didn't fool around—"

"Because I wasn't fooling around. My job was to meet you."

"To harass me."

"I'm going to stop you, Mr. Cameron. Your old tricks aren't going to work. I think you're just as scared of all the things that scare everybody else."

"You don't know a damn thing about me."

"I know a lot more than you think." Honey seemed to catch herself. "Everybody's scared, Mr. Cameron. Even..." She paused, trembling slightly, perhaps because his powerful body was edging closer. Her gaze slid up his dark rugged face. "Even bullies like you."

"Is that what you think I am?" he demanded quietly.

"That's what you just said you were. Nell said so, too, but... I—I think, or at least I *hope*, that you could be very nice if you wanted to be."

His gaze touched her eyes and then her mouth. "And your special mission in life is to manipulate me to be nice?"

"Manipulate is your word."

"Changing me is an impossible mission."

The light of the sun was in her mussed hair. Her determined lips parted into that infectious smile.

He drew a deep breath. "Honey, you're in way over your head."

Her defiant smile caused his pulse to quicken. He started to say something cutting and found he couldn't.

Hell, he was swimming in deep, uncharted water himself.

Her smile vanished. Fear had replaced defiance in her eyes, and he wished it hadn't.

He liked her.

Not that he understood this sudden, incredible affinity he felt for her—a stranger. Nell's manager. His adversary.

Besides that, she was poor and he was rich. He knew all about being poor, all about what men and women would do to better their cash flow. He had been chased by lots of women who were after him just for his money, women who wanted to use him. Usually he used such women—as long as they pleased him.

Her tongue slid out to trace the dry outline of her soft pink mouth. She drew away from him, shaking her head. "We should be natural enemies." A red tangle fell softly against her cheek.

His breath caught. His eyes were fixed on her mouth. "Baby, if you're smart, you'll run."

"I can be foolish sometimes. Besides, I have a job here."

His immense frame eased closer.

She swallowed. Then she looked over her shoulder uncertainly at the Filbert Steps. "But who says it's a crime to follow sound advice?"

She took a single faltering step away from him. Then she made a wild, defiant dash across the porch.

But he was faster.

He caught her by the wrist and eased her against the wooden wall of her house, his body pressing into hers, his hands and arms securing her against him as she cried out softly, trying to free herself.

"I thought you told me to go."

Women were easy for him. It had been a long time since he'd had to chase one. Something wild and dangerous was smoldering to life inside him, something that had been dead for years. "Maybe you're too tempting to resist."

She balled her hands into fists and pushed at his chest. Her eyes blazed with defiance.

He lifted her chin and stared into her eyes' hot, burning light, which so turned him on. He crushed her effortlessly to him, her breasts pressing against his wide chest, her hips pushing into his thighs. A fierce white heat consumed him. Every movement of her body as she struggled against him brought fiery surges of pleasure.

But his voice was gentle. "Honey... Honey, I'm not going to hurt you."

Very slowly she stilled.

A vast silence seemed to envelop them as he held her. Her face seemed lost, devoid of all hope. He, too, felt overwhelmed by the same bottomless despair. Instinct told them that each had the power to annihilate the other. And yet neither of them wanted to run.

She stared up at him without breath as he flexed his big brown hand and brought it slowly toward her to smooth the wayward red tangle away from her soft cheek. Then his rough-textured fingers traced lower, along her satiny, high sculpted cheekbone, down the slender curve of her warm golden throat, lingering against her quivering heartbeat before he turned her face gently up to his.

"I've never known a woman like you."

Her frightened, luminous eyes held his. Again she seemed to stop breathing as he continued to explore every inch of her face.

Like one mesmerized, Honey watched the slow descent of his mouth. The instant his lips touched hers, he felt her quicken. As he deepened his kiss, he felt her arms slowly come around his neck, her fingertips tightening reluctantly against the corded muscles of his back as she arched herself nearer.

She accepted his tongue when he flicked it inside her lips. Her velvet mouth was hot and moistly delicious.

She was everything he had imagined and more—hotly alive and tenderly naive, all at the same time. One kiss, and wildfire raced through his veins.

More than anything, he wanted to carry her into the house
and have her naked and writhing on that green bed beneath
him. He imagined her nipples, budding tight and hard
against his mouth. He knew she would be good—better than
those piles of fancy skeletons he'd been sleeping with for
years. He was a man who usually took what he wanted
without a qualm.

Instead, even when every cell in his body throbbed to have
her, he relaxed his grip and let her go.

What the hell was wrong with him?

All he knew was that he felt different with her.

Alive. Almost human.

He drew in a deep, ragged breath and then let it out in a
long, frustrated sigh. "What is going on here?"

Too weak to stand, she sank against the wall and laughed
shakily, a little hysterically. "It's called animal attraction.
Instant chemistry. I never believed in it before."

It was more than that.

"Dangerous stuff," he muttered fiercely, running a light
finger across her lips that caused them both to shiver.

"The kind of chemistry I teach to seventh graders is pretty
tame," she said.

"Then it's nothing like this."

"No... I—I wish it hadn't happened."

"Some things can't be undone."

"Mr. Cameron, please... You're the last man I would
choose to feel like this about."

"Thanks."

"I—I know what you must think of me. What any man—
but, especially a man like you—would think."

"A man like me..." He felt a smoldering cynical fury.
Toward her. Toward Nell, who had obviously thoroughly
brainwashed her. For the first time in a long time he regret-
ted his nasty reputation. "I doubt that you do."

"Nothing like this has ever happened to me before."

"Likewise," he said very coldly.

Her golden skin reflected the pink light of the sinking sun. He looked at her passion-swollen lips and despite his anger, he felt as if he were starving for them.

He wanted to taste her again, and not just her mouth. He wanted her hands on his body, too. But she wasn't the kind of woman who could endure the easy kind of passion he had in mind. There was an intensity about her, a true innocence in her soul that even he, jaded though he was from a hard life and too many easy women, didn't want to despoil. Not just for her sake but for his own. Because he would hate for her to despise him when she learned what kind of man he really was.

"I don't want this to happen again," she said.

"Neither do I." He ran his hands through his unruly black hair that had tumbled over his brow. "Baby, if you're smart, you'll stay away from me."

"Because your intentions are not honorable?"

He set his hot, insolent eyes on her until her lips quivered with fright. "Nothing about me is honorable, Honey Rodriguez."

"Do you always warn women away?" she asked, her voice husky with fear

"Not usually. Take another summer job. Anywhere but here."

"I—I can't do that."

"It will be dangerous for you—living near me. I usually take what I want. And I want you, Honey Rodriguez. But you're not my type, and I probably wouldn't be interested very long."

A twinge of genuine hurt and then fright crossed her white face. "You were in a hurry. I'm sorry I kept you so long."

"My pleasure— Honey." He smiled wolfishly.

Silently, she walked to the Filbert Steps. He followed right behind her.

As they ascended the wooden steps together, he did a curious thing. He picked the fat yellow rose she had admired and gave it to her.

"You shouldn't pick the flowers. They'll wither and die sooner than they should," she said quickly. "You should leave them for other people who come after you to enjoy."

"I've picked a lot of flowers I shouldn't have picked—for my own personal pleasure. I've never given a damn for those who came after me."

As she took the rose, she caught the dark note in his voice and knew intuitively he wasn't talking about flowers.

"Do you believe a man can change, Miss Rodriguez?"

"If he really wants to."

"Then you are not as cynical as I."

"I wouldn't want to be."

He did a second curious thing. He never confided any of his personal problems to anyone. But he found himself doing so—with her.

"I was upset when I found your note."

"I meant to annoy you."

"No... My teenage daughter was expelled from her private school this afternoon for some very unladylike conduct, conduct that I'm deeply ashamed of because of my own background... or rather my lack of proper background."

"That's probably why she did it. Kids always go for the jugular."

"Well, I was proud when my daughter was accepted to such a classy school. Then when she told me about this crazy thing she did, I felt like wringing her neck."

Honey smiled at him, her fear gone. "That's a normal impulse. But don't do it. Be kind. Try to find out what's troubling her. She probably just wanted to get your attention."

They had reached her car. Joshua opened her door and she got in.

"I'm afraid I'm not very good at kindness. I didn't experience much of it growing up. And I haven't spent much time with her. You're probably good with kids."

"Not always."

"I grew up on the street. I've tried to give her everything I never had, but she throws it all back in my face and rebels."

"Then she's a normal teenager. Don't give up on her, Mr. Cameron. That's the main thing."

"I never give up—when I set out to do something."

She started her car. "Neither do I."

Twilight had fallen, and he noticed that she had begun to shiver.

She held out her hand in farewell.

"Then you'll heed my warning and stay away from me?" He took her hand, knowing deep in his heart that the last thing he should do was touch her.

Her green eyes were unreadable. "Goodbye, Mr. Cameron."

"Joshua," he murmured.

"Joshua," she repeated, but very softly and a little defiantly.

There were no words to describe how good he felt when she said it. There was no way he could resist leaning into the car and kissing her goodbye, either. When she tried to pull away, he wouldn't let her.

His kiss was soft and gentle and possessive, and after it was over they were both more afraid than ever.

Six

―――

"Midnight, get me a list of the casualties!" Joshua strode grimly beyond the steel deck of the new high-rise tower he was erecting as an expansion of his hotel.

With the grace of a cat, he sprang across the naked girder and stared down through the unfinished walls and floors at the ruin of concrete walls and the overturned crane many floors beneath him.

Midnight was a few feet behind him. "No casualties, J.K. You were lucky as hell. When the crane collapsed, the crew had shut down for the day."

Joshua turned and saw his own profound relief mirrored in Midnight's jet gaze. They'd both seen too much violent dying to ever forget the pain that went with it.

Back in his office an hour later, secure in the knowledge that no one had been hurt, Joshua fought to concentrate on what Midnight and his architect were saying. What frustrated the hell out of him was that he'd been distracted at work all week.

Joshua was glad when Midnight and the architect finally left. Maybe he could pull himself together before either of them came back and bombarded him with more legal or architectural problems.

Joshua got up slowly from his desk and went to a window. The city beneath was silent like a dead dream city. He watched the cars glide through the downtown with quick, quiet purpose. He watched the Golden Gate Bridge disappear as fog rolled in from the Pacific. He saw sailboats on the bay and felt the need to get out on the water himself. He wanted the icy wind on his face; he wanted to breathe in the tangy smell of the sea. Impossible—he never took off in the middle of the week.

He felt trapped in his glassed-in cage, lost, not himself. He ran his hands through his black hair. He hadn't been worth a damn ever since he'd met Honey Rodriguez one week ago.

Not that he'd seen her again. She'd avoided him as though he had a fatal disease; she'd done exactly what he'd said he'd wanted.

Damn it. Why couldn't he forget her? Why did he keep remembering the way she'd smelled? The way she'd tasted? Why did her sweet, defiant smile continue to haunt him? Why couldn't he work with his usual ferocious energy? Why did he search every narrow side street on Telegraph Hill for that green monstrosity of a car every night when he drove home? Was he crazy? And why did he feel like he'd met her before?

A man with his problems didn't have time to moon over a woman like some lovesick teenager, especially a woman so totally unsuitable. He had had constant hotel-renovation and construction hassles. Then there had been all the frustrating dead ends with the Brazilian project. The Wyatt takeover wasn't going well, either. Only today he'd found out that Hunter's wife had blocked him from buying more Wyatt stock.

How the hell an amateur like Mrs. Wyatt had scraped up enough cash, lured in a partner and financed the purchase of that run-down casino hotel in Vegas, he would never know. But since Joshua already owned the maximum number of casino hotels he could own by law, he couldn't take over her chain, without selling one of his own highly profitable casinos. He'd been stopped—cold. By a woman. He remembered Wyatt's daughter and realized she'd made good on her threats.

His own daughter, Heather, compounded his business problems by making his time off a living hell. She was even moodier and more argumentative than she'd been after Monica had first left them. When she wasn't hysterical about some tiny problem, she fought with him constantly.

Two nights ago he'd blown up at her for watching a trashy television show at two in the morning. She'd yelled back, refusing to listen when he told her that if she stopped staying up till dawn and sleeping through lunch she'd feel better.

Not that she ever did anything worthwhile when she was awake. She did her long blond hair, which stayed lank and stringy no matter how many hours she combed it, or she listened to awful music and talked incessantly on the phone. When he'd offered her a part-time job, she'd refused to work in his office.

In desperation he'd decided that she had to go to summer school. He'd insisted until she'd sulkily agreed—if she could pick the school. Then she'd made the worst possible choice by selecting one nobody had ever heard of, just because it was near the house and she could walk and make friends with the neighbors.

She constantly criticized him.

Joshua didn't like thinking about Heather, so he went back to his desk and tried to work. When he hadn't finished by seven, he crammed a briefcase with hotel blueprints and went home anyway.

In his kitchen sink he found the remnants of Heather's soggy peanut-butter sandwich. He ate alone and went up to his office, spread out his blueprints and resumed work. He'd just begun to really get somewhere when Heather's choked voice came from the door, interrupting him.

"I know you don't want me here, Daddy."

He looked up. She was dressed sloppily—in a big black T-shirt and black shorts. *He hated black on kids.* He hated the way she didn't know how to dress yet. Her forlorn blue eyes were glassy bright and huge; her complexion was mottled with livid red spots. Her blond hair was untidily plaited into a crooked French braid. She was at that coltish stage—too skinny and long legged. She was ill at ease with her newly budding feminine body. She didn't know what to make of herself, and neither did he.

She needed a mother—to help her dress, to do her hair. To help with the other important stuff.

"I know you don't want me to bother you, Daddy."

He damn sure didn't. His hand clenched around his pencil.

"I was trying to work, Heather," he said, deliberately keeping his voice calm.

Her bottom lip quivered. "I know I'm just in your way."

How the hell was he supposed to answer that? He couldn't say she was right, so he'd said nothing.

"When Mother went away I felt I was less than nothing, that I had no one."

A frown crept into his eyes. That's the way he'd felt, too. Not that he could admit it. He set his pencil down carefully and raked his hands through his hair.

"Why did Mother leave me and then have a new baby when she won't even let me come see her?"

Hell, she left me for another man.

Heather's tear-filled questions filled Joshua with rage against Monica. His fingers tightened against his scalp.

"Daddy—"

"For God's sake, don't ask me about your mother."

"You won't ever talk about her."

His mouth thinned. His bleak eyes stared at Heather, almost hating her when she came to him like this, pleading and in tears, because she reminded him too much of Monica and all the hopeless years he'd wasted with her.

"Did you ever love her, Daddy?"

He shoved his chair back from the desk and got up. Striding across the room, he threw open the glass doors and plunged out into the cold, damp air that brought the salty smell of the sea.

His hands gripped the balcony railing as unwanted memories of his ex-wife deluged him. The brutal truth was that he'd married Monica for her money and family connections. Not that he hadn't tried to make their marriage work. Monica had been a spoiled socialite who'd considered herself better than the poor bad boy from the bad neighborhood she'd found herself curiously attracted to, though she'd married him anyway. He'd thought she was class. She was pregnant before either of them realized he hadn't held her values. Not that they both hadn't been climbers. It was just that they were clawing their way up different ladders.

He hadn't understood her fierce competitive desire to establish them in society by spending their entire lives at endless parties he'd considered silly. She hadn't understood why he worked so hard in his own business when she had all the money in the world. He hadn't known how to play up to the kind of people she considered socially important, people who made him feel empty, bored, unsure—inadequate. Not wanting the same things, they had torn each other apart. In the end Monica had left him for someone with old money.

"I'm leaving you because I've found a man with real class," Monica had thrown at him as she'd slammed the trunk down on her suitcases and punched the garage-door opener. "You're still just a cheap hood who hasn't learned that money isn't class."

"Oh, I learned, Monica," he had said softly, edging menacingly closer to her in that shadowy garage, causing her to panic in that last moment and quickly jump into her car and snap her door locks. "Maybe you shouldn't be too hard on a cheap hood just because he was attracted by your shallow glitter."

When Heather made some soft sound as she stepped out onto the balcony, too, Joshua was jerked back to reality. He forced himself to relax his hands on the railing. Monica was gone. For good. She had a new family now. He turned toward Heather wearily. All he wanted now was to forget Monica and live in peace.

But Heather wasn't about to let him. "Why did Mother leave us, Daddy?"

"Damn it! Don't push me."

Her young, unhappy face crumpled. "Why?" Her one word was a desperate plea.

"Because of me. Because she thinks I still stink of the gutter I was raised in."

"She's not like that."

"If you don't like my answers, don't ask me questions."

"Why can't you ever be a real father? Why can't you ever...just once...make me feel better—the way Midnight does?" A strangled moan escaped her lips.

Because he didn't know how. Because he wasn't talented the way Midnight was with kids. Joshua swore in a brutal, frustrated undertone.

"You always hurt me," she whispered. "Always."

"Damn it, Heather. What the hell do you think you do to me?"

"But I don't want to hurt you, Daddy. I want to be with you."

Her pleading eyes held on to his for a painfully drawn out minute. A tear slid down her cheek. She waited as if she actually expected him to touch her, to comfort her as Midnight would have done. But a dark bitterness stole over Joshua. When he just stood there she backed slowly away from him, sobbing as if he were a monster.

"Heather—"

He followed her as far as the darkened circular stairwell and listened to her footsteps flying down the stairs. He flicked on the light so that she wouldn't stumble on a stair.

Her door slammed and he turned the light off again, glad to be alone once more. It was no use going after her. She was right. He'd been hurting people so long, he didn't know how to do anything else.

Inadvertently a perverse thought struck him. Honey Rodriguez would know what to say, how to be kind and patient and understanding.

Damn Honey Rodriguez. She'd avoided him.

He went back to his desk and stared down at the blueprints. All he could think of was that he longed to see Honey—again.

He cursed viciously. He felt out of control, furious. With a single frenzied swipe, his brown hand raked across the desk, sending blueprints, notepads, pencils and pens flying. Then he stomped over the jumbled sheets, not caring that he ripped one of them on his way out to the terrace.

He barely saw the glittering blur of the Oakland Bridge, of faraway lights across the bay. The garden four stories beneath him was dark. He drew in a deep ragged breath. He had to get himself back in hand.

Muted laughter drifted up from the garden, and he looked down, seeking anything that might distract him. A pair of lovers embraced tenderly on the Filbert Steps in the shadows beneath the palm tree. The sight of them made him feel even crazier and more alone as he stood on his empty terrace and looked down on a city of hundreds of thousands. When he wrenched his gaze away from the entwined pair, a golden light snapped on—high up in Honey's apartment building.

Her light. It seemed to glow brighter than all the other lights in the world. Joshua's pulse accelerated.

He held his breath when, a few minutes later, Honey came to the window and stared up at his house for a long moment. His breathing became labored and harsh as he imagined her eyes seeking him in the darkness. Slowly, almost reluctantly, she lowered the shade.

He watched her window anyway. Even with her shade down, he could see her moving about. Suddenly she came close to the window again. Her shadowy womanly form was silhouetted in the center of that golden rectangle as she began to undress for bed.

He stood statue still, unable to stop himself from watching her. When she grabbed the bottom edges of her knit shirt and pulled it off over her head, his heart began to beat violently in his throat.

He watched her strip off her shirt and toss it carelessly onto the floor. Lazily she began to run a brush through her hair. He imagined its silkiness, its fire flashing against her slender neck. When her fingers came around her back and unhooked her bra, he began to shake.

Her breasts swung free. Dear God. The sight of her, knowing that she was half naked behind that shade, rocked his senses. He ached to hold her, to touch her, to know if those shapely breasts felt like warm velvet. He shuddered, his pent-up emotions in violent upheaval as he viewed the shadowy curve of bosom, waist and the voluptuous swell of her hip. The memory of the time he'd kissed her moved through him like electricity.

She was such an alluring mixture of defiance and fear and sweetness. More than anything he wanted to call her, to hear her voice, to talk to her—just one more time.

Only when she turned out the light was he released from her spell. Only then could he go back inside and pick up his phone.

He set it down again—hesitating. He felt insane with some fierce male need to claim, to conquer, to possess. But he would only hurt her.

Was it his ghetto breeding that made his blood run hot and wild despite his decision to be noble? Or was it just because he'd told himself he couldn't have her that he wanted her so much?

His fingers tightened in a stranglehold around the receiver. Then he set it down and pulled a slim black book out of his drawer.

Instead of Honey, he dialed Simone and asked her out for the next night, hoping sex would help him forget the woman he *really* wanted.

Joshua's date with Simone was the final disaster of his disastrous week.

Instead of taking her to bed, he took her home after dinner and told her goodbye forever. The next morning he had his secretary shop for a very expensive parting gift for Simone. He opened the black velvet box, scribbled a terse goodbye and his initials on a crisp card, inserted the card in the necklace's center and snapped the box shut.

Simone called the moment she received the diamonds.

But not to thank him.

"Who's the lucky girl, J.K.?" Her voice was husky, knowing, amused.

"My daughter's moved home."

"There's more to this than your daughter. You're different."

"In what way?"

She laughed huskily. "Not so sure of yourself. Perhaps, *cheri,* this time you've met your match. I'd like to meet the new woman."

"Simone—there is no new woman."

"Really? Why don't I believe you, J.K.?" Simone hung up laughing at him in that infuriating way that reminded Joshua of Midnight.

Sharks die if they don't keep swimming forward.

Dark suited, paisley tied, Joshua marched into his office Monday morning determined to let no distraction stop him from moving forward, determined that he was done with dwelling on the past and the absurd desire he had for a woman who was all wrong for him.

He glanced at his watch impatiently. He had a meeting with Midnight—they were supposed to go over the legal problems of the Wyatt takeover. But Midnight was late.

Suddenly from outside his office, he heard Midnight's laughter. Ticia giggled. More warm laughter from Midnight.

Midnight was never too busy to take time for women. Even though he hadn't devoted himself to one woman in particular for years.

The door swung open and Midnight stepped inside. He was holding a glass of iced cola. Sensing Joshua's dark mood, Midnight's smile died instantly. He set his drink down on a sunlit table.

"You're late."

"I got a ticket. The cop gave me a long lecture. Then I got hung up up at the hotel, too." Midnight yanked off his black leather jacket and tossed it onto a chair. He shrugged toward a boy of about nineteen who was lounging in the doorway behind him. "Come on in, kid. No matter what you've heard, Mr. Cameron has probably had his breakfast. I don't think he'll eat you alive."

"Thanks for the character reference, Midnight," Joshua growled.

Midnight shrugged. "Anytime, J.K. Kid, I said come in."

The haggard kid behind Midnight was dark and tall and unshaven. His old jeans and even older-looking running shoes made him look poor—ghetto poor. He moved in that faintly edgy way rangy kids from dangerous neighborhoods moved, head down, hands out of his pockets. His eyes were older than the rest of his face, and he took in everything with quick, restless glances even though he didn't dare stare.

"Meet Tito Pascale," Midnight said.

Tito shifted uneasily, lowered his black head and stared at his grubby shoestrings. There was an ugly yellow bruise beneath his left eye. His lip was cut and swollen.

"Why should I bother?" But Joshua was interested in spite of himself.

"He works for us, and he works twice as hard as the next best welder we've got. He's from our old neighborhood."

"Memories from the old neighborhood hardly warm my heart."

"So? What does?" Midnight smiled grimly.

"Midnight, are you going to tell me what the hell's going on here?"

"Tito wants to take off for a few days. His mother's sick."

Joshua studied the kid's black eye and swollen lip. "You know my policy, Midnight. I fire people who lie to me and demand special favors. I'm running a business, not a charity. We're behind on construction. I'm not some softie who can afford to fold at every employee's petty demand."

The kid broke in. "This is life-or-death. I swear I just need two days, Mr. Cameron. I like my job. I need it. I can't afford to lose it. My mother—"

Joshua leaned forward. "It's bad taste to lie about your mother to get something you want, kid. You've been in a fight. You're in some kind of trouble. You gonna tell me what your real problem is?"

The kid would have run, but Midnight had edged himself between the boy and the door. "You came here to talk to Mr. Cameron," Midnight murmured.

For an instant the kid looked desperate and lost. "I can't tell you, Mr. Cameron. I need the time. You've got to help me."

"I don't help people."

The furtive eyes grew resentful as they moved swiftly from Joshua's face across the plush opulence of the mauve office. "I guess you've been rich so long, you've forgotten what's it's like to be poor—to be someone like me."

Joshua went white. His body tightened. He turned away abruptly, but not before a terrible rush of the old helplessness swamped him. He felt the kid's hate. Hell, it felt like his own.

"No," he said quietly. "I haven't forgotten."

"Mr. Cameron—" The boy's fierce, desperate voice came from behind Joshua. "I've gotta have the two days to find my mother a new place to live. My stepfather beat her up bad—she looks worse than I do. He took everything we had. He's said he's coming back with a gun. I've got to stop him."

Joshua felt slightly ill. The kid would rob, maybe even kill, to get the money he needed—if someone didn't help him. He would kill his stepfather too, if the guy really came back and pushed too hard. Joshua knew because he'd been there. Only he'd been lucky.

Joshua turned around slowly. "Okay, kid. Will you get out of here if I give you your two days and enough money so you don't have to do anything crazy?" Joshua pulled a checkbook from his pocket, ripped out a check and scribbled on it. "This is a loan. It's not charity."

The kid took the check and eyed the amount. His eyes flickered with new hope and then an even fiercer determination. "I promise I'll pay it back."

"With interest. But use it to stay out of trouble, kid."

Midnight watched the stunned kid back out of the room. Then with a half smile he turned back to J.K.

Joshua spoke first. "You find that jerk of a stepfather and bring him here—to me."

"Will do." Midnight's smile broadened.

"What the hell are you looking so pleased about, Midnight?"

"You tell me, J.K."

"He came to you for help, didn't he, the way my men always get around my rules by going to you—because beneath your tough exterior you're a sucker for their sob stories? Why didn't you help him yourself? Why did you bring him to me?"

Midnight shrugged, lifted his cola to his lips, sipped and frowned. "Must be a warm day. The ice seems to have melted in my drink." He hesitated thoughtfully.

"What the hell were you doing, Midnight, bringing that kid here?"

Midnight set his drink down. "I was checking you out. You've been different ever since you tangled with Wyatt's daughter. Softer."

"Damn it. Soft is the last thing I want to be. You know what I went through better than anyone."

"Other people have it just as bad."

"I don't give a damn about other people."

Midnight's eyes grew darker. He edged closer. "That's always been your main problem, J.K. I'd just about given up on you until lately."

"I'll be back to normal soon."

"You call hating everyone that lives and breathes on Mother Earth normal. Hey, don't change on my account. I like the new you. But what I can't figure out is how Miss Wyatt got under your skin when you never even went out with her?"

"Cecilia Wyatt has nothing to do with it."

Midnight stared at him, clearly puzzled.

The old Joshua never confided. The new Joshua surprised them both. "There is someone though—a woman, who's been on my mind."

"That's great."

"It's hell!"

"Who is she?"

"A redheaded neighbor of mine. Nell's new apartment manager. But it's over." Joshua took a quick breath. "Hell, it never even started. She's not my type."

"Call her up, J.K."

"No!"

"Then give me her number and I'll call her. I'm not as big a snob as you when it comes to women."

"You stay the hell away from her!"

Joshua looked dangerous and jealous. His hard voice held that threatening note Midnight remembered from their leaner, meaner days.

But Midnight just laughed as he lifted his glass in a mocking salute. "It ain't over with you and her, boss," he murmured. "Not by a long shot. I'll lay you fifty to one that she's melting your heart faster than the sun melted this ice."

"Go to hell, Midnight."

"Hey, that's where we both got our start, remember? No way am I going back. Not even for you." As always Midnight clung stubbornly to his point of view. Grinning, he grabbed his jacket and slung it over a broad shoulder. "Call her, J.K."

Seven

Why did the Bomb have to die today of all days?

Honey almost felt like crying as she lifted the grimy phone from her Chinese mechanic's filthy counter and called Mario. She still couldn't believe Foon Lew wanted five hundred dollars to fix the Bomb.

Mario didn't answer till the seventh ring, and at first all she heard was the pounding of his drums. Then he mumbled hello and grunted indifferently when she told him their problem.

"Mario, we don't have five hundred dollars—" *Why was she trying to explain? Mario lived in his own world—girls, his music, his motorcycle, his job, school—in that order.* "Just come get me," she said at last, hanging up in frustration before he could protest.

Honey went wearily over to her car. The Bomb was jacked up. All she could see of Foon Lew were the frayed cuffs of his blue jeans and his dirty tennis shoes sticking out from the front end.

"Foon Lew, please, isn't there something cheaper you could do? I don't have five hundred dollars."

"Then you don't have no car."

Her redheaded parrot, Emerald, began to dance on his perch in his huge cage which she'd set on the garage floor. "You don't have no car. You don't have no car."

Honey leaned down to her bratty bird and pinged a fingernail against his cage. "Be quiet." Her voice was schoolteacher firm.

For once Emerald obeyed and pecked docilely at his perch.

Foon Lew jumped out from under her car. "You want car fixed?"

Honey had to pace for a minute. The shop was so noisy she could barely think. From one corner a radio blared rock and roll. The concrete floor was so littered with tools, she almost tripped over a tire iron. Tattered photos of Foon Lew and his sons on their fishing trips fluttered from tacks on the walls. The place reeked of grease and gasoline.

She stopped suddenly, opened her purse, and got out her checkbook to inspect her dismally low balance. The magazine with Joshua's photograph on the cover fell out. A faint tremor went through her when she found herself staring into his brilliant ice blue eyes. Just his picture brought a melting wave of emotion that was so strong she felt she could reach out and touch it.

Her trembling fingertips brushed his lips. Then she swallowed on a deep, anguished breath, slammed the magazine shut and threw it back into her purse. She was so upset, she forgot to check her bank balance.

"Okay, Foon Lew, you can fix the car."

He smiled, very pleased.

She would have to charge the repairs. The thought depressed her, but not as much as thoughts of Joshua did.

If only she could solve her problem with him as easily. Her shoulders slumped as she picked up Emerald's cage and walked outside to wait for Mario.

She had moved to Telegraph Hill to confront Joshua, to stop him. Not to hide from him. But for ten days she'd parked at the bottom of the hill and climbed the steep Filbert Steps, deliberately using the back way to avoid him.

And the reason she was scared was because she'd expected him to be a monster and she'd found out he wasn't.

Dear God. It was worse than that. She knew she was crazy, but everything about him drew her—both his fierce ruthlessness and his gentleness. One angry kiss and she'd wanted to stay in his arms forever.

She'd married Mike to prove she wasn't some spoiled, little rich girl. When he'd died she'd buried herself alive and pretended she was in love with his memory. Joshua made her feel wild and vibrant and young; he made her feel real— honest. One kiss and she knew how unbearably lonely her sham of a life was.

Honey had wanted to discover J. K. Cameron's human, vulnerable side. Instead she'd discovered her own.

Now her father wasn't the only one in danger of being destroyed by J. K. Cameron.

He was a seducer of women, and she ached for him to ply his skill. There was no way she could help her father without risking herself.

The roar of Mario's powerful motorcycle broke into her troubled thoughts. She stepped out onto the curb and flagged him.

Dust and bits of paper garbage swirled as the big bike braked, skidding to a terrifyingly abrupt stop one inch in front of her. Flying rocks hit Emerald's cage and the parrot danced and squawked in frantic terror.

Two teenage girls in miniskirts squealed delightedly, impressed.

"Show-off," Honey accused.

Mario ignored both the admiring girls and the parrot. He took off his helmet and flashed Honey his warmest male smile, as foolishly pleased with his dashing arrival as she was annoyed by it.

"What took you so long?" Honey asked, lifting Emerald's cage from the ground.

Mario was stunningly handsome, having inherited the dark good looks of his beautiful Italian mother. He had olive skin, a white-white smile and auburn hair. He was all too aware of the effect he had on most teenage girls. He shook his head and his thick mane of dark hair—which Honey was always after him to cut—shone with red highlights as it rippled to his shoulders.

"Sorry I'm late. I stopped off to get you something." He unzipped his leather jacket and pulled out a torn paper sack. "Hungry?"

When he handed her a freshly baked croissant, she realized she was starving. Only when she began to eat the moist warm bread, did he bother to smile nonchalantly at the girls.

"I ate three of them," he admitted which didn't surprise Honey. Mario had been eating like a horse since he was ten.

"Did you go to your classes today?"

Suddenly tense, he looked away uneasily. "Not to English."

"Mario! What am I going to do with you? You can't major in girls—" She bit back a nagging maternal lecture—one he'd heard already countless times and remembered her new plan to be more positive with him. "Thanks for the croissant and for coming so quickly. Now remember, you've got to drive slowly because of Emerald."

Mario relaxed and handed her a helmet. "Because of you too. Tell me, am I supposed to park at the bottom of the hill again tonight and walk up?"

The thought of running into Joshua filled her with dread as she reluctantly eased herself onto the back of Mario's bike. With one hand she held onto her purse and Emerald's cage. She slipped her other around Mario's waist.

"No." She bit her lip. "Let's park at the top."

His dark head jerked around. He whistled admiringly. "So, you're finally going to beard J. K. Cameron in his den?'' Mario stomped his boot down hard on the gas several times. "Brave lady."

The motorcycle roared and then rocked backward. Honey strangled a scream as the big bike jumped out in front of a garbage truck.

A taxi honked—swerving at the last moment.

Brave lady—Mario had that right.

A big black motorcycle revved its motor and shot past Joshua's low-slung sports car, streaking recklessly up the steep grade of Union Street.

"Idiots! Heather, you're not to be stupid like that girl and ride behind some leather-bound madman on a motorcycle!"

Heather who'd been sulking ever since Joshua had picked her up from school and taken her to the grocery store, snapped to attention. She was mad because he'd refused to let her have a friend over for the night.

The motorcycle stopped ahead of them at a red light. Joshua pulled up right behind the couple. The punk kept revving his motor. A pretty girl in a pink ruffled dress waved at him from the sidewalk.

Heather sighed. "Anybody would ride behind him, Daddy. He's pure hunk. Wow!"

Pure hunk! Did Heather say things like that just to goad him? She didn't have the vaguest idea what guys like that were like. What they were after from girls. At least he hoped she didn't.

Instead of snapping back at Heather, Joshua disciplined himself to taut silence. His grip tightened on the leather steering wheel.

"Daddy—"

Joshua ignored his daughter. They were only a few blocks from the house. It seemed safer to let his gaze wander to the voluptuous hourglass figure of the girl in the green shorts on the back of the motorcycle.

A wisp of silky, shiny red hair fluttered from beneath her black helmet against her skintight green knit top. Why, the kook was even holding a huge bird cage.

There ought to be a law. There probably was—in California.

The light changed. The biker and his girl raced up the hill. Tires screaming, they made a quick left on Montgomery Street.

Joshua made the turn as well and was surprised when the biker parked in the vacant space right behind his own garage.

The girl got off first and set down the bird cage very carefully. She seemed a bit shaky as she stretched. She had shapely legs. Slowly she took off her helmet.

Her glorious tangled hair gleamed even redder in the afternoon sun. When her dazzling green eyes met his, she started.

He should have known.

Honey Rodriguez! He recognized her instantly, staring at her for a long, silent time until she looked agitated and a little afraid. Staring at her until the bones in his hard jawline bunched painfully. He forced his gaze away from her tight, flushed face.

He was hurt. And surprised. His profound disappointment felt like a fist jammed hard in the gut.

Almost immediately his unwanted emotions jelled into hatred for her and her muscle-bound punk.

She could do better, Joshua thought disgustedly as he punched his automatic door opener.

She could have had me.

No, she couldn't.

Joshua couldn't believe that he'd nobly resisted her because he'd thought her wholesome. Then she went for a kid, a punk biker.

The punk had taken off his helmet and was leaning over his bike. He had pretty hair that fell to his shoulders. His arms were brown and muscular. He appeared all of twenty-two.

"Boy!" Heather said. "Would you look at that?"

"What?"

"The hunk—cute, huh?"

Joshua felt fresh horror when he realized Heather was staring fixedly at Honey's muscle-bound companion.

"I wonder where they live, Daddy."

The punk was done with his close inspection of his motorcycle. He eased himself up off his muscular haunches. Heather waved wildly as he did so and he waved casually back, his dark eyes appraising. Then he gallantly picked up the heavy bird cage and put his other hand against Honey's back to escort her down the Filbert Steps.

Joshua bristled with rage at the way the punk had looked at Heather, at the way his possessive brown hand had nudged the small of Honey's spine in such a free-and-easy fashion, as if he thought nothing of touching her.

Joshua stepped on the gas and swerved into his garage, punching his automatic door opener to close the second they were inside.

He turned angrily, "You're to leave that guy alone, young lady. He's already got a girlfriend."

"She's way too old for him, Daddy."

"Sweetheart, you've got that right."

From his kitchen window, Joshua could see the bay. He also had a clear view of Honey's bedroom window.

Joshua wasn't looking at the bay.

Nor was he paying much attention to the filet mignon smoking on his grill. Nor to the two potatoes he was microwaving. Neither he nor Heather liked microwaved potatoes, but neither of them was much good at real cooking.

Joshua tore his furious gaze from Honey's window and went to his liquor cabinet where he poured himself a drink—straight scotch on ice. Lots of scotch; not much ice. The scotch had been a gift. He'd kept it around to serve his guests because he rarely allowed himself a drink.

Heather's wild rock music throbbed loudly two stories beneath him. Usually he hated her music. Tonight he liked the way it pulsed angrily in his blood.

The light in Honey's bedroom window came on, and as before Honey came to her window and stared up at Joshua's house for a long minute. Then the young punk joined her there. She turned slowly, touched his face with deep affection. They talked passionately for a long moment. A muscular brown arm pulled the shade down. And the shapes of their bodies lingering against the lighted shade drove Joshua mad.

Had she let that young punk move in with her?

Joshua downed his drink and poured himself another. He bolted it too, and it hit his empty stomach and burned through him like acid. He didn't like to drink because it unleashed his demons and made him remember his father and how bad things had gotten before he'd shot himself.

Her bedroom light stayed on. From time to time two shadows loomed against the shades. He tried not to imagine what they were doing in there together. It was very late when the light went out and Joshua tore his gaze from the window. By that time he had burned their steaks and had drunk way too much.

As he climbed the stairs to his office, he felt faintly sick.

And mean.

Very mean.

Eight

Joshua felt worse than mean the next morning. He was queasy from a hangover, and his brain felt on fire as he grabbed a cup of black coffee, the newspaper and the thick stack of legal papers dealing with the Wyatt chain that Midnight had prepared. Joshua dragged himself slowly up the winding stairs to his terrace.

Before Heather had moved in, he'd gone to his office Saturday mornings. Now he worked at home.

Heather's friend had come over anyway last night—right after dinner. Her father had driven off, dropping her at the door, suitcase in hand, before Joshua could object. Since he'd been in no condition to drive the stranded girl home, Heather had won another battle.

Joshua sat down at his patio table and scanned the newspaper. A headline at the bottom of the front page caught his attention.

Sam Douglas Shot
Lacy's husband.
Midnight's Lacy.

This could change everything.

Sam would be no loss to the world, Joshua thought bitterly. Then he thought of Lacy. Maybe she wasn't as cold and self-serving as Midnight believed. Maybe she'd really loved the bastard.

Joshua read the article. Most of it dealt with Douglas's accomplishments in the senate and the ongoing investigation into his murder; apparently his mentally disturbed son, Cole, was being sought for questioning. Only the last sentence made faint mention of the fact that the assets of the Douglas estate had been frozen while the Internal Revenue Service looked into Sam's financial affairs. There seemed to be some question concerning the misappropriation of money from Sam's campaign fund.

Lacy was the only woman Midnight had ever loved. She'd seemed like an angel until she'd jilted Midnight for Douglas. Midnight had never gotten over her.

Still, Joshua wondered if she needed anything. He would call. Midnight would be furious if he found out. Damn Midnight. Lacy had been Joshua's friend, too. She'd had it tough, the same as he and Midnight had. Maybe she'd had her reasons for doing what she'd done. Regardless, Joshua had to know if she needed anything.

He set the paper aside and began to flip through Midnight's highly detailed documents that dealt with the legal complexities that might arise over air rights, massive construction contracts, tax easements and disputes regarding the environmental consequences of several of Wyatt's hotels.

Joshua yawned. Midnight was thorough, too thorough at times. It would take all day to get through the papers, but the house was quiet. So was the neighborhood. Maybe he'd be able to concentrate.

But the girls got up—way before noon, hours earlier than he'd expected since they'd played music long after he'd gone to bed. All too soon the smell of chocolate-chip cookies baking in the oven distracted him.

Chocolate-chip cookies were his favorite. But for breakfast? He smiled in spite of himself, wondering if Heather was cooking them especially for him. With an effort he forced his attention back to his work.

A few seconds later a frustrated male yelp from the Filbert Steps distracted him again. When the yelp was followed by a crash, Joshua set down his coffee and leaned over the railing. An open guitar case was sliding down the wooden steps. Honey's punk boyfriend was leaping down the stairs three at a time like a great agile monkey.

Joshua snorted in cynical amusement and gulped down more coffee.

Then he saw the boy's weights, his big guitar and his drums stacked on Honey's front porch, and the hot black coffee ate into his empty stomach. The boy was moving everything he owned into Honey's apartment.

For a minute Joshua couldn't breathe. He felt an indefinable element of disappointment right before his temper skyrocketed out of control.

Joshua leaned further over the railing and watched with a jealousy-crazed mind. Which was absolutely absurd. Joshua had told her he never wanted to see her again.

He clenched the wrought-iron railing. *He'd lied.*

He remembered Honey's marvelous eyes, her flame-silk hair, her lush body. It didn't seem to matter that she wasn't glamorous, that she couldn't possibly fit into his life. He wanted her.

He'd wanted to save her from himself. But not for some punk who would be even worse for her than Joshua was.

Honey's bedroom shade was still down. Joshua thought of her lying there in tangled sheets, her fiery hair disheveled from lovemaking, still asleep, waiting for...that boy.

Joshua's mouth went hard and thin.

His headache sharpened and he felt even sicker at his stomach. He was about to grab his papers and go inside when Honey's mongrel cat scampered up the fire escape and leapt out onto the table, plopping himself squarely on top of them. Mr. Right flattened his ears and asserted his squatter's rights with an arrogant meow.

Joshua scowled down at the scruffy animal. The big cat's green rhinestone collar sparked back at him as brightly and defiantly as Honey's eyes.

Joshua was poised to rake the foul beast off the table when he heard Heather's bright giggle from the steps below.

Joshua raced to the balcony edge again. To his horror he saw that Heather and her friend were knocking on Honey's front door. The girls were scantily dressed in bright miniskirts and holding a sumptuous platter of *his* homemade cookies.

Interested, the long-haired punk swaggered slowly up the stairs and joined them on the porch. He set his empty guitar case down beside his drums and took a cookie. Several cookies. As he chewed, he eyed the girls with equal enthusiasm. He obviously had abundant, voracious appetites. Oozing charm, he leaned closer and said something that made both girls giggle. Then he held the door open, and the three of them disappeared inside.

Rage consumed Joshua.

It was bad enough that Honey was wasting herself on a boy who was obviously going nowhere. But Joshua wasn't about to allow his daughter to do the same.

There was nothing left to do but go after Heather.

Joshua pounded loudly on the wooden door. Mr. Right howled with equal determination. The damned beast had had the audacity to follow him.

From behind the door Joshua heard the soft padding of footsteps. Then the front door was gently opened. He caught the faint odor of fresh paint.

Honey's big, surprised green eyes met his. "Hi," she said, smiling, before she panicked and backed away from him.

Joshua drew in a deep breath, suddenly rigidly ill at ease too.

Honey stood barefooted in the doorway, masses of gleaming wet hair flowing like a river of flame to her shoulders. She was wearing an emerald-colored robe that came to her ankles, and she smelled deliciously of perfumed soap and shampoo. In one hand she held a half-eaten green bean which she was offering to a gigantic green parrot with a red head. The bird was prancing excitedly on her shoulder. In her other hand she held the last bit of a chocolate-chip cookie.

Damp, fiery tendrils were glued to Honey's forehead; more of them clung to her neck. She was so enchantingly sexy looking, so fresh and lovely, Joshua had to force himself to remember he was not glad to see her, that he had come for the sole purpose of laying claim to his wayward daughter.

"I see you've brought Mr. Right," she murmured. "I saw him climbing up your fire escape."

The parrot nibbled at the bean and then spit out his bite onto the threshold and shook his head disgustedly. The cat sniffed at it with equal disgust.

"Oh, dear," Honey said, concerned. Then to Joshua: "Emerald's been very sick. He has stress molt from the move."

Joshua warmed to the bird. *So, the parrot didn't like the bike or the biker, either.*

"I've been cooking all his favorite foods—pinto beans, corn—"

The parrot strained toward her cookie, and she gave it to him.

"I guess I didn't need that anyway." Honey smiled at her bird and then looked up appealingly at Joshua. "Why are you here? I thought we were off-limits to each other."

"This isn't a friendly visit," he said, remembering why he'd come.

Her eyes widened again with fear.

"Oh. Then I'd better take my cat and shut the door."

Joshua held the door open with his hand. While she tried to force it closed, Mr. Right dashed inside. Honey looked startled. The bird began to squawk.

Realizing her strength was nothing against Joshua's, Honey let her hand fall from the door. "What do you want then?"

His insolent gaze devoured her body and then returned to her face. She was paler. Her wide eyes stared uncertainly into his. She looked like a doe at bay, fearful that the predator was closing in for the kill.

"I came after my daughter," Joshua said grimly.

Honey sagged against a wall, a little of her tension easing. "Oh. The girls came down to welcome us into the neighborhood. They took Mario on a walk."

"So, his name's Mario?" Joshua sneered, coming nearer. "Mario what?"

Her voice quivered. "Rodriguez."

Joshua towered over her. "The same as yours?" His gaze fell to her left hand. For the first time he saw the wedding band glimmering there.

"His mother was Italian. His father, Hispanic." Her frightened whisper was barely audible. "Sometimes that adds up to a volatile combination."

"Rodriguez—you're not married to that macho punk?" Joshua's voice had grown even colder.

Honey laughed shakily, beginning to understand him at last, but too incredulous to take him seriously. "Married— to Mario? Don't be absurd. He may look mature, but he's still very young."

"Oh, so he just lives with you?"

Puzzled, she looked closely at Joshua. "You think that Mario and I—" she broke off awkwardly, confused, distraught.

"Naughty boy," screamed the bird.

"Excuse me." Honey's voice was quick and urgent as she dashed toward the bird's cage. "When Emerald says that, he needs to go back to his perch over newspaper."

The bird jumped dutifully onto his perch.

"Why does he live with you?" Joshua had followed her inside. His hard eyes slid over her with fresh contempt.

Her back was to him. "Who? Emerald?" Her voice was too casual. "I told you—I like pets."

"Mario! Damn it. Why does he live here?"

She turned around very slowly. "Because he's my step-son, and I've taken care of him since he was a little boy," she said quietly. "My husband, his father, died two years ago. Mario's had some problems. If I hadn't kept him, he would be out on the street. I know he looks kind of wild, and his sole ambition right now is to be a rock star. But if you look past the bike and the long hair, if you can stand the drums and his friends, he's a terrific kid."

"What were the two of you doing in your bedroom till all hours last night?"

"Were you spying on me?"

His question was louder. "What were you doing?"

"See for yourself!" Furious, she spun away from him and opened her bedroom door.

The scent of new paint filled the room. Joshua saw fresh white walls, apple green windowsills and baseboards and a protective layer of paint-splattered newspapers spread over her bedroom floor. His eyes returned to her indignant white face and lingered there for the space of another heartbeat.

Slowly his anger began to drain away. "You were painting—"

She pulled the door closed.

"You look too young to be his stepmother."

"I was too young when I married Mike."

Feeling very foolish, Joshua sank down on her couch. Even though he was too embarrassed to look at her, at the same time he was wild with relief.

Not knowing what to say or what to do, he studied the scuffed floor for a long, awkward moment. He had grossly misjudged her. There was nothing to do but to collect Heather and go.

Honey's soft voice filled the tense silence. "Mario has girlfriends his own age—lots of them. I think you owe me and him an apology."

Joshua started guiltily. At the same time he was non-plussed that she had assumed the upper hand so quickly.

She came to him and leaned down, her sweet-smelling body temptingly, dangerously near. "It was obvious you were thinking the worst of me."

He didn't bother to deny it, but he didn't bother to apologize either.

"I'm surprised you were so morally outraged," she said, needling him and bending even nearer. So near, he caught the scent of jasmine and fresh soap. "I mean you're the last person I would expect to be shocked by the thought of a woman taking in a younger lover."

"I wasn't upset." He kept his black head lowered and ground out the lie harshly.

"Then why did you barge in on me with that I-could-kill look on your face?"

"Because I was worried about my daughter."

"So, you came down here...only because of your daughter? That's probably why you just happened to notice that Mario and I were busy in my bedroom for hours last night."

"Damn it. Why are you pushing me? I was determined to stay away from you. I know you're wrong for me, and I'm all wrong for you. You know it, too."

"Yes," she said in a sad, small voice that somehow he knew would haunt him long after he'd gone. "Yes, I know it, too."

But on some deep level she wasn't so wrong. And she made him feel crazy with the way she was standing so close to him wearing that robe and maybe nothing underneath it. So crazy he couldn't stop himself from reaching up and putting his hands around the back of her waist. His jealousy was gone, but in its place was a mushrooming need.

Her muscles tensed. She drew in a deep, desperate breath, but the light pressure of his fingers around her waist was so gentle and undemanding she didn't struggle.

"Relax," he murmured, anguished longing in his tense voice. "Just relax."

"That's hard to do around you."

Slowly, silently he drew her closer and buried his head against her belly. For a long moment he pressed his face hopelessly against the soft green robe that covered her stomach.

He felt the delicious heat of her. Her sweetness enveloped him and filled him with fresh longing. He ached to pull her down on his lap. To kiss her. To do more.

Gingerly one of her hands came down to caress his thick black hair. Warm fingertips moved hesitantly over his brow.

"Joshua, I wanted to see you, too," she admitted in a low, shaken tone that sounded sad and lost. "I look up at your house sometimes, too."

She was every bit as afraid as he was.

"I'm sorry," he said. "For what I said. For what I did."

"For what you thought," she whispered.

"For what I thought," he admitted.

She laid her hand against his cheek for a long moment. Her fingers were warm and light, irresistible. He turned his head and blew a kiss into her open palm. She jumped back, startled, as if he'd jolted her with an electric current. He felt a thrill in the pit of his stomach—as if they'd connected in some body-to-soul way.

"You probably date someone beautiful," Honey said in a small voice.

Joshua looked up at her for the first time. "Not any more."

Honey stood very still. "Why not?"

"Because I don't want to."

"So, what do you tell a girl you don't want any more?"

"Goodbye."

Honey's exquisite eyes were fastened on his dark face.

"Look," he muttered guiltily. "She wasn't hurt. We weren't in love. She understood."

"You don't seem like the kind of man to do without a woman for long."

"I don't do without anything I need—for long. Does that bother you?"

"A lot of things about you bother me," she said.

"Yeah . . . I hate myself most of the time too." He got up slowly to go. "When Heather comes back, tell her to come home."

Honey nodded stiffly. "You don't have to worry about Heather and Mario. She's not his type—I mean not that way. He goes for more sophisticated girls."

Not his type. Joshua's gaze locked with Honey's and he felt his blood heat. *Somehow that was hardly reassuring.*

Joshua was at the door when Honey awkwardly switched the subject. "I—I was wondering if there's someone new in your life. I mean . . . a new woman?"

He shot her a quick look, and she blushed, as if aghast at her boldness.

Her interest in him was so transparent that he couldn't help smiling faintly. "I'm afraid there is."

"What's she like?"

In the soft light Honey's eyes sparkled with fire. Her silky, damp hair clung to her graceful neck.

He bared his teeth in a seductive smile. "She's very lovely—in her own way."

"Who's the lucky girl?" came that sweet, sad, lost voice.

Simone's words. They made him hesitate. "Don't you know?" Before he could think, he crossed the small room in a single stride and folded her hand into his.

Their fingers touched, mating hotly like fire and water shot through with electricity. When he pulled her to him, he felt her shiver. He wanted to kiss her hard on the mouth, to open her robe and kiss her everywhere, to taste hot, voluptuous woman flesh. But she had some quality that made him feel vastly out of his element, that made him go much slower than he wanted. So, he just looked at her delectable lips for a long moment and then into her eyes.

"Do you sail, Ms. Rodriguez? I keep a boat at the yacht club—"

"Mrs. . . . I told you before that I'm a widow." She turned her face away as if the thought of her dead husband still upset her.

"Yes . . . I remember that now." Gently Joshua touched her chin and tipped her face nearer his, so that he felt her breath, hot against his skin. "Are you still grieving? Is that why—"

Her long lashes flickered. Guilt darkened her eyes. "I haven't dated anyone. Not since my husband's death." She was trembling. The fear was back in her voice. "Mike is only one of the reasons why I don't think we should become involved."

Joshua lifted her left hand and studied her ring silently for a long time.

"Right," he whispered bitterly, letting her go. "I shouldn't have asked you."

In that first moment of total rejection he felt hollow.

Women had said no to him before, but it had never felt this awful.

Thank God his pride saved him from begging her or from saying something utterly stupid. Thank God he just walked silently toward the door and shoved it open.

A cool, damp wind blew inside.

Her parrot squawked. Honey called Joshua's name, but he went out onto the porch. Up the wooden stairs. Away from her.

It was only later that he was aware of the awful expanding emptiness inside him, of the deep and burning need for this woman that was so all-consuming there was no room in his heart for anything else except the bleak, cold knowledge that she didn't want him.

Nine

Joshua's throat was dry and painfully tight as he edged restlessly nearer the window of Tito Pascale's new apartment to check to see if that skinny kid he'd paid to keep an eye on his car was still there.

His car was his escape out of there.

The kid was leaning against a lamppost sucking on a Popsicle in the foggy street. Joshua's elegant black sports car was still down there. So was the litter and filth and the broken glass on the sidewalk and in the gutters.

His old neighborhood. The fog made it seem worse. Why the hell had he come—even for this brief, perfunctory visit? Just the short drive through the narrow dilapidated streets had brought the past back, brought the terror of that time when he'd felt he was less than nothing—when there had been a threatening thug on every street corner ready to take him on.

Even now, when he knew he could return to the wealth and security of his new life, he felt that some part of him had never escaped. For an instant he was so harrowed by the old trapped hopelessness, he felt almost laid naked by it. He remembered the terrible time after his mother had died—the foster homes, running away, living in filthy back alleys for days at a time. Would he ever really get away from his past?

Joshua gripped the freshly painted windowsill and then forced himself to release it. He dusted his hands on his jeans.

Idiot! He was safe now, or at least as safe as anyone could be. He had everything he wanted.

Then he thought of Honey, her fiery loveliness, her mystery, her passion. Most of all he remembered her rejection. His mouth thinned in a tight, unhappy line.

He forced his mind from her, back to the Pascales. At least they seemed happy with the way the interior of their apartment had turned out. The place was small, but it was clean. And they were safe now from the man who had threatened them.

Joshua had loaned Tito the money for the new paint and furniture. He'd dealt with the stepfather by paying him to leave San Francisco for good, by giving him a chance to start over in Vegas and warning him not to come back.

"I've gotta go now," Joshua said abruptly to Tito and Mrs. Pascale as he moved away from the window to the door.

They joined him there, clinging to each other, their faces shining with happiness and hope and pride in their new home. Joshua grimaced at the thought that Midnight would probably ride him forever about this and might expect more good deeds. But for the moment, Joshua didn't care.

"We'll never be able to thank you." Mrs. Pascale pressed Joshua's hand as he opened the door.

Joshua felt embarrassed by their gratitude. He hadn't done much, but then a little went a long way down here. To Tito he said, "Any more problems—you come to me. No more fights. And you enroll in night school like you promised."

"Yes, Mr. Cameron."

The Pascales shut the door slowly, smiling after him until he reached the stairs.

After the new brightness of their apartment, the hallway seemed damp and crumbling. In the dim light of a bare low-wattage bulb, Joshua saw the depressing gloom of peeling paint and moldy wallpaper. He strode carefully because of the sagging wooden stairs. The banister was loose. On a lower floor a shadow moved in a darkened corner and Joshua tensed, instantly alert to danger. He sighed with relief when he saw it was only a rat skittering across the floor.

Joshua remembered the congestion of his childhood, the lack of facilities, the cold and the unreliable water supply, the rats, the roaches, the indifference of landlords, teachers and the outside world.

Most of all he remembered the way his mother had given up and died—four years after his father. After that Joshua had lived on hate. He might drive away today, back to his safe, clean neighborhood, but he knew that deep down he could never really get out—and all because of Hunter Wyatt.

His thoughts were black as he stepped out into the chill of the foggy street. The last person he expected or wanted to see was Honey Rodriguez driving slowly by in her chartreuse Bomb looking for a parking place.

He stared after the green abomination with surprise and fury and not a little fear. Then he started running after her.

Was she crazy to come down here alone? She was driving so slowly, he easily caught her. *Anybody could have.* He lunged out in front of her bumper and slammed his hands—palm open—against her fender.

She braked and honked. When he yanked her unlocked passenger door open, a chemistry text tumbled out. He caught it before it hit his foot and heaved it onto the back seat, which was messily crammed with a dozen boxes, filled with books, manila folders and student notebooks.

In her soft green knit blouse and skirt, Honey looked pretty amidst the jumble of boxes. Too pretty to be down here alone.

He was curious, but more than curious he was possessively angry. "What the hell are you doing here? And why
the hell don't you lock your car doors?"

Her green eyes flashed back at him. "Nice to see you too,
Joshua."

"I asked you a question," he growled.

She lifted her chin and stared defiantly down its pert
length at him. "I'm going to my school to store some stuff
that I don't have room for in my apartment."

"Where is your school?"

"If you must know, it's right around the corner."

"You teach down here? This is a dangerous neighborhood."

"It's not *that* dangerous. I've worked here ten years. A lot
of nice people live here."

He grimaced. "I grew up here."

"See what I mean about nice people," she said lightly.

"I'll drive you to your school."

"The last thing I need is you around, acting like everyone you see is a criminal."

But before she could finish he had walked around her car,
opened her other door and gotten in.

When she threw up her hands in a gesture of mock surrender and scooted out of his way, he smiled grimly across
at her. "What if I was a bad guy? You'd be in real trouble."

Every sensory receptor in his body flashed red hot at her
languid look.

"Maybe I already am," she said softly.

"You should lock your doors," he warned gruffly, snapping his own lock. "I mean it."

"Are you always so sure you know everything?"

The instant he slammed his door, he knew he was in just
as much danger as she was. He caught the scent of jasmine
and felt a primitive, hot-blooded response at finding himself locked into such a tiny space alone with her.

And she knew it.

His hands gripped the steering wheel. "So why the hell do you have to teach these kids, Honey?" he asked bitingly, keeping his fierce eyes on the street because it was too dangerous to look at her.

"They need me more than some kids do. Because there's a losing battle going on in the streets of our big cities and in their schools, and I'm trying to save as many kids as I can. It's hard, more frustrating than I can say, but someone has to show them there's a way out."

She'd hit a raw nerve with that one. He stomped down hard on the accelerator. "Honey, there's no way out. And there's little chance that someone like you could show them the way if there was."

"You got out," she whispered.

He laughed derisively. "Did I?"

"You're successful."

"It's all surface. I'm still running, Honey. Make no mistake about that. And hating." He eased the car around the corner. "The hate stays forever."

She pointed at a dingy red two-story building on their right. "There's my school."

"There's a parking place."

"It's too small."

"No problem. The one thing San Francisco will teach you is how to park." He touched the turn signal. "Nobody ever really gets out," he persisted as, despite her objections, he began the seesaw process of parallel parking her large car into the tiny space on the steep hill. "Nobody. Do you understand me? The ones that do—they're like me—they just pretend they do." He paused, concentrating on backing the car for a moment.

She gasped as her fender slid past the bumper of the car in front of them with less than a millimeter to spare. "You almost hit him!"

"A long time ago I thought I could," he continued. "But all the self-hate, the despair, the misery, the desire for vengeance against anyone you can find to blame—it sticks. It goes deep, deeper than anything else. Deeper than all the nice things that happen to you. You don't ever forget places like this. You take them with you. No matter how high you climb, you can't escape it. And you can't ever fit in anywhere else. I believe in hate, not love. In saving myself, not others. In taking all I can and giving nothing to anyone. People like me keep people like these down here, but if these people had the chance they'd stomp on me too."

"Joshua, you don't have to be like that."

She was an idealist. You couldn't reason with idealism.

He put the car in park and set the emergency brake. "Feed that line of garbage to your students, Honey." He cut the engine and smiled. "I told you the space was big enough."

She wasn't about to feed his ego. "Barely... I do try to encourage them."

Two lean, ill-kempt teenage boys with narrow, restless eyes rode aimlessly down the middle of the street on battered bicycles. When they saw Honey, they waved and she waved back.

Bitter memories from his youth made Joshua frown. "But I bet the kids know better?"

"Some of them think they do, the way you say you do. They act tough, the way you try to act tough."

Did she think this was a game? Furious, he tore the keys from the ignition and dropped them into her outstretched palm, careful to avoid touching her. "It's not an act. You leave your real life somewhere else when you come here. That's something none of us can ever do."

Her trembling fingers closed around the keys. "I take this home with me at nights, too, Joshua."

"You have a choice though. I don't."

Careful to keep her eyes lowered, she edged nearer her door.

Away from him.

He wanted to seize her, to pull her back. To forget this ridiculous too-personal conversation.

"Maybe you're not so tough, Joshua. Maybe you're just scared like a lot of the kids I teach. Maybe you just want love and safety... and..."

Yeah. He'd wanted those things. He still did. His stomach twisted in knots.

She touched his shoulder hesitantly, and her unexpected warmth sent a shaft of desire through him.

"Maybe it's not too late... even for you, Joshua," she said ever so softly.

He seized her wrist. When she recoiled, he let her go in disgust.

"And who's going to give them to me—you? You can't wait to get away from me."

"Maybe if you weren't biting my head off at every opportunity, I wouldn't feel that way." She leaned quietly toward him again, and he was aware of her dizzying scent as she picked up her purse and put her keys inside it. "Thanks for parking my car. And thanks for the dog-eat-dog pep talk." She bent down, her breasts swaying against soft cotton. "I guess it's goodbye for now. I've got real work to do. I'm sure you do too."

He felt on fire with frustrated longing. "Yeah, you're out to save the world and I'm out to destroy it." He gazed cynically at the filthy neighborhood. "Looks like I'm a hell of a lot better at my job than you are at yours."

She picked up a heavy box of files from the floorboard and put her hand on the door handle. Hesitating, she forced herself to look at him.

His blue eyes were so savage and hot she gasped.

"Joshua," she said faintly. "It's easy to give up on life. That happens everywhere, not just down here. You could change, if you really wanted to. But only you can do it. Maybe you already have and you don't like it. Quit feeding your hatred and your desire for vengeance. You're a very talented man. Live your life positively."

Hatred and vengeance were the last things on his mind at the moment. Her red hair was on fire. So were her eyes. *So was he.* He wanted to drag her into his arms and silence her with his lips.

"You make it sound so easy, but you don't know what you're talking about," he muttered, struggling to sound coherent. "The world's full of two kinds of people—winners and losers. Quit wasting your time on losers."

"Which kind are you?"

He stared at her hard, almost hating her because he'd sworn he'd leave her alone.

"Why do you enjoy holding such a cruel view?" she asked, misinterpreting his expression. "Not just of this place but of yourself? Is it so wrong to believe we can make the world a better place if we try? That we can be better people if we try to be? That we can make neighborhoods like this safer places?"

"It's not wrong," he said in a hoarse, low tone. "But it's cruel to feed it to kids down here."

"Cruel? How?"

"Why feed people dreams of a fairy-tale world they can never be a part of and wouldn't like if they were? They're better off the way they are."

"Then why were you so determined to get out?"

"It was easier for me because there was a man I was determined to destroy." His mouth was drawn into a grim, forbidding line. "I couldn't take him on when I was poor, because I didn't have the right weapons to finish him off."

She had begun to shiver, and he realized he'd gone too far. All she said was a quick, "I've gotta go."

But he knew she meant—goodbye for good.

It was for the best.

The hell it was.

Before she could open her door, he dashed around to her side and helped her out. "You little fool, do you think I'm going to leave you down here alone?"

"Really, Joshua. I don't want you here. Not after—" Her face was very white, her tone cool, while his own heart was pounding crazily. "I mean I've got to carry all this stuff inside and store it. It's going to take a while. I'm sure you're way too busy getting revenge on the world to have the time to help me.''

He seized the box she was holding. "I'll make the time."

She tried to wrest her box back. "Look, this is ridiculous. I want you to go."

"I told you I'm not leaving you down here alone."

Her green eyes smoldered. "There's no winning against you, is there?"

"Not when I really want something," he told her quietly, a hot challenge in the dark look he gave her.

"Look, I thought I made myself clear Saturday—"

"Very clear!" he snapped, remembering her rejection. "Don't flatter yourself. You're in no danger from me—not in that way." *Liar.*

She picked up another box and marched away from him in hostile silence. He smiled grimly, stacked several more boxes on top of the one he had and followed her inside.

He was setting his stack down on her desk in the front of her empty classroom and about to go after more, when her quivery voice stopped him.

"I'm surprised you'd even care I was here. I would have thought that by now you'd already have a new girlfriend."

His gaze jerked swiftly to her white face. "So—what if I do?"

She arched an eyebrow and tried to look merely casually interested, but she was too still.

He felt a bolt of warm excitement, a half-formed hope as he hesitated before replying. "Would you care?" he demanded arrogantly.

"No, I—I was hoping you'd found someone—so you would leave me alone." But her lashes fluttered and she wouldn't look at him.

He felt a powerful hunger to go to her, to touch her, to pull her into his arms and assure her there was no one else. But it was smarter to let her wonder. So he left her inside her classroom and went out to bring more of her things in. It took her an hour to arrange everything in storage the way she wanted it.

When they had finished, she sat down at her desk to write in her calendar. He tried to act casual as well and went out and got a drink of water from the water fountain in the hall.

She made the mistake of following him.

She stood right behind him, so close that he felt her body's warmth, so close he caught the smell of her fragrant perfume. When he was done, she took her turn. He watched her bend gracefully over the porcelain fountain. Sunlight slanted through a high window onto her fiery hair, which fell all over her shoulders. He watched the water glisten against her soft, wet lips. He studied the way green cotton molded her body.

The fierce need to touch her was too much. His hand shot around her and he eased her against his body. Her soft warmth set him on fire. When she gasped, he leaned over her and whispered into her ear, "Baby, if I forgive you for last Saturday, will you date me?"

She tried to jerk herself free of him, but he held her fast, liking the way her every movement ignited sparks in him.

"You said I was in no danger—if I let you stay."

"If that's the only lie we ever tell each other, we'll be luckier than most," he murmured, savoring the sheer, unadulterated pleasure of holding her.

She paled. His hands tightened, and he pulled her harder into his body. Her lush, warm legs slid against tough thigh muscles. She set him aflame.

"I'm not skinny. I know you like skinny—"

He was blistering hot. "Hey, I like you," he whispered. "You feel good. Too good."

"Joshua, no," she murmured breathlessly.

"Someday I want you to say yes in that same breathy voice."

"I never will."

He laughed knowingly. "I'm too conceited to believe that."

His amusement seemed etched in every carved line of his face, but he let her go—unfolding his big hands slowly. When she was free, she stood trembling for a long moment. There was no sound other than his own pounding pulse. Then she scampered away from him into her classroom. She was gathering her purse and her notebooks from her desk when he stepped inside.

He stood grimly at the door, blocking her only escape. Carelessly he flipped the dead bolt. Her horrified little cry echoed in every corner.

He laughed softly. Their eyes met across the shadowy room. Hers were wide and alarmed; his burned with a hot, expectant light.

"Joshua, no—"

He strode toward her. "Yes."

"Not now. Not here."

"Now," he whispered huskily. "Here."

Even as she began backing away, he stalked her, grinning when she darted this way and that, trapping her easily against the blackboard behind her desk.

"You're through running," he rasped. "So am I."

"Are you out of your mind?" She tried to twist out of his grasp.

His iron fists closed over her wrists and he lifted them high against cold green slate. Chalk dust crumbled to the floor. "I told you this was a dangerous neighborhood."

She moaned and turned her head away. "You only want to go to bed with me."

He smiled insolently. "Would that be so awful?" His deep voice had softened dangerously.

Panicked, she kicked at his shins, little knowing that every time her leg rubbed his powerful thighs and torso she sent fresh waves of hot excitement charging through him until he was so wild it seemed unbelievable he could want any woman this much.

His whole body tingled. "Baby, if you're smart, you'll stop doing that," he muttered in a fierce, shaking voice. "You're just turning me on."

She stopped instantly, but his body was already as hot and hard as a brick fired in a kiln. His uneven breaths were more ragged than hers.

"You and your materialistic, self-serving values and your quest for revenge are everything I've spent my life running away from. I never want to see you again. Do you understand me?" she cried, her own breath heavy and hot and sweet against his throat.

"You think you're so noble, so different from me," he taunted, pulling her closer, so that his muscled body seared her softer flesh. "But, Honey, I wonder." He threaded his fingers through her hair and forced her face nearer his, so near that her lips were a mere fraction of an inch from his. "I think you're as attracted by my dark side as you are repelled by it. You get a vicarious thrill out of slumming down here with people who are toughened because they have to live on the edge."

"No." But she was breathless. Her eyes were glued to his lips as if she were mesmerized. She drew her tongue cautiously along the edge of her parched mouth.

"No?" He laughed. His warm fingers touched her throat and her fluttering heartbeat there. "Your pulse is beating even faster than mine. You like this jungle, Honey. You're too real yourself, too alive to be the saintly type you pretend you are. You like the jungle wildness in me. Because it's in you too."

"Let me go."

"Besides, if I'm such a lost soul, and you come to the jungle to save souls, maybe you can save mine."

"I want you out of my life." But when she looked at him, the hunger in her gentle eyes sent a different message.

"Do you?" His fingers moved down her throat. With expert ease, he began to unbutton her green knit blouse. His hand slid inside her lacy brassiere to cup her breast, to knead a velvet nipple until it grew pert and taut. He laughed again at her body's quick, involuntary response. "I think you're a liar. If you really wanted me out of your life, you wouldn't have moved onto my hill when I warned you not to."

"*Your* hill? You arrogant, conceited..." At his slow, erotic kneading of her nipple, her voice grew faint, dying away.

"I never pretended I was perfect."

"Please—don't—" she muttered shudderingly as his hand moved over her belly and he molded her body to his. Frantically she dug her fingers into the hard muscles of his arms and strained to push him away. And yet he knew she wasn't really fighting him.

"You should have escaped when I gave you the chance." He felt hot, hard and pulsating. His nostrils flared. "You know the kind of man I am. Sooner or later, I always take what I want. And I want you."

"You don't. Not really."

"Yes. I do." He lowered his black head toward hers. She would have turned away, but he caught her chin and held it still. Then his mouth came down on hers, his tongue sliding across the soft fullness of her lower lip, demanding admittance. After that his ravishing kiss seemed endless to them both. With his lips and tongue, he took possession of her mouth, of her.

"You're beautiful, so beautiful," he whispered. "You can't fight me any more than I can fight you."

Their mouths joined again. Their tongues mated. Slowly, surely, his deepening kisses saturated her with the same fiercely hot rapture that ensnared him.

"Joshua. I feel like I'm throwing my whole life away, but I can't stop myself."

"I'm not going to hurt you," he whispered.

Her hands touched his raven hair uncertainly. She ran a caressing fingertip down the hard length of his cheek and jaw. Then she locked her arms around his neck and arched her body willingly into his powerful muscular frame as if she craved the same total oneness with him that he craved from her. She was with him on this ravaging journey—all the way.

Her response made him hungrier than he had ever been, and his mouth left her lips to kiss the rest of her face, her brows, her nose, her ears. Then he pulled her soft knit blouse apart and brought his head lower, suckling each voluptuous breast hungrily in turn, tasting honey soft, ripe flesh, until she was as wildly hot and breathless as he, until he knew nothing mattered to her more than his touches and kisses, until he was sure that she was filled with the same keen delight and exquisite excitement that filled him.

A mad darkness seemed to swirl around them. He was whispering things to her he had never said to any woman. He was feeling emotions no other woman had ever made him feel. Honey tried to speak, but his mouth closed over hers again. And as he pulled her down, down into that thick blackening, destroying whirl, he sensed that he had lost something of himself, too.

"I'm afraid," she said.

Strangely, he was too.

Their hotly fused, shaking bodies slid against the black-board wall to the floor. Joshua knew a wild need to have her, to take her.

To conquer. To possess. To make her his. Forever.

Now. On the cold tiled floor of her empty classroom.

As he held her crushed to him on that hard floor, she sighed in soft surrender. He felt himself shudderingly near the edge—almost crashing over it as if he were being swept in the violent surge of an avalanche.

"Do you know something crazy?" she whispered gently, her big eyes glowing with a strange, rapturous light. "I've never felt like this about anybody. I'm afraid of you, but I'm more afraid that I'll never feel like this again."

Use or be used. Take or be taken.

She was sweet. She almost made him feel sweet when she looked at him like that.

His old philosophy jarred.

His hands retraced the path from her shoulders to her breasts, and her little shiver of delight thrilled him too.

Outside two kids screamed and began to bounce a bas-ketball against the brick wall. Joshua heard the ball thud again and again. At first the dull, repetitious vibrations seemed far away and no part of his hot, sensual mood. Only slowly did that change.

He pulled so hard at her blouse that a button came loose. He watched it roll across the floor, and as he did he became aware of what he was doing, of how hard and cold the floor they were lying on was, of how rough he had been. He opened his eyes wider and saw the badly scarred legs of Honey's big wooden desk, the rusty casters of her chair. He forced his gaze up to the dusty blackboard, to the tattered edges of the world map that hung on the opposite wall.

She was an idealistic teacher who wanted to help poor kids. This was her classroom. He admired her.

He picked up her button and turned it over in his palm. The cold reality of what he had done, of what he was about to do, sank in.

As he looked down at her, he thought her lovely with her eyes passionately closed, with her lashes still against her sensually flushed cheeks, with her delicious lips expectantly pursed. Her soft breathing was irregular. For a moment he watched the gentle rise and fall of her breasts. How trustingly innocent she seemed.

A great tenderness welled up inside him. She was too lovely to take, to exquisite to use.

He didn't want to stop. He wanted to make wild, violent love to her. He couldn't, because she meant more to him than he understood.

He kissed her fiercely and then gently. When her whole body arced with abandoned longing, her hands tightening on his body, he knew that she was as highly roused as he. But she was too sweet to defile on the floor of her empty classroom.

She began undoing the buttons of his shirt. His hand closed over hers, stopping her. For a long moment neither of them moved.

Then he tore himself free and lunged a safe distance away from her to lay doubled over against her desk, his fists clenched, panting in an unreal state of tortured frustration and pain. At the same time he felt a burning desire to crawl back and take her.

If she'd come to him, if she'd touched him or spoken to him, he would have lost all control.

Instead she leaned against the tiled beige wall beneath the blackboard, staring at him with blazing hurt eyes while her nerveless, shaking fingers slowly buttoned her blouse and fumbled to smooth her tangled hair.

Then she got up like some bewildered wild thing and ran from the room—from him—as if she were suddenly terrified for her life.

Ten

_____

She was terrified of him. Because she was so on fire for him.

Honey's heart beat in sharp, pounding little throbs that seemed to vibrate painfully in her temples and fingertips. Two hours had passed since she'd run from Joshua, but the memory of the way she'd willingly ended up on the floor beneath him burned her with shame.

Even in the silent peace of her own home eating her favorite kind of chocolate bar for comfort, she felt threatened. Both from Joshua and from herself. From the knowledge that the sacred memory of Mike's love would never be enough to satisfy her again. She wanted more.

She wanted Joshua. She wanted to soothe away his anger and his pain, to bring out his gentleness, to know the wild thrill of his passionate lovemaking.

Why had he let her go? He had told her the kind of man he was. Had his punishing kisses been nothing more than a warning? Was he giving her one last chance to escape?

It was a lazy, ordinary summer afternoon. The fog had vanished, and the bay was glistening sapphire blue in the sunshine. On his perch near a screened window, Emerald preened green wing feathers, stopping occasionally to stare at the tiny new apples dangling temptingly from a low limb by the window. Tail flicking, Mr. Right was watching Emerald through slitted eyes from the windowsill. Mario was outside on the porch tuning his guitar, getting ready to sing something he had written to Heather and to Tina, one of his girlfriends.

Honey was wondering how she could want a man who intended to destroy her father. A man who would deliberately destroy her, too, when he discovered who she was.

When her teakettle whistled, she gathered her two candy wrappers for the trash and got up from her couch like a zombie. Clumsily she brewed tea in her favorite china cup and went into her bedroom where she set it down and forgot to drink it.

She looked out her window up at Joshua's house and her eyes filled with a sort of shrinking dread. He was standing on his terrace, his long legs spread widely apart, as he stared down at her, his blue eyes hotly searing.

The instant he saw her, he backed away from the ledge. She jumped back just as quickly, fighting her panic, snapping the shade down so that he couldn't watch her, so that she couldn't see him either.

When she returned to her living room, she felt no safer. She couldn't erase the knowledge that he was up there—waiting for her, wanting her. Nor could she erase the memory of the heated glory she had known in his arms, of the hurtling sense of pleasure he had given her.

Nothing in her marriage had prepared her for the dark, frightening power of Joshua and the passion he ignited in her. And Joshua knew it.

Mario began to sing. His melting, smoky baritone intensified the ache of longing in Honey's heart. Honey wanted to go outside and shout to him to stop. She wanted to order Heather home and tell her never to come back. And yet in the same moment that Honey arose, she sank once more to her chair, helplessly torn, not only because she liked Heather but because she sensed that the motherless girl was lonely and hurt and in need of real friends whom she could trust. But at the same time Honey hated to encourage the child of her most dangerous enemy. When the truth of their relationship became clear, Heather would only be hurt again. No, Honey must encourage Heather to try to become close to her real mother.

The longer Honey sat in the darkened stillness of her living room, the more hysterical she felt. Her plan to tackle Joshua on a personal level had been hopeless from the start. Not only had she put herself at risk, but she was endangering Heather who was too fragile to sustain another betrayal. Not to mention the very real danger of how Joshua would retaliate when he discovered Honey had deliberately tricked him.

She saw now that her move to Telegraph Hill had been a mistake. The only smart thing to do was to call Nell and quit this charade before it was too late for them all.

Then the phone rang, and the instant she heard the shaking vulnerability in Joshua's husky voice, her fierce resolve to leave him melted like butter over a hot flame.

"Don't hang up," he whispered in a low, anguished note.

She was powerless to do anything other than listen.

There was a long moment of silence.

"I'm sorry...about this afternoon," he said at last. "For the way I treated you."

"It's all right," she said weakly. "I—I'm not proud of the way I acted either."

"You have nothing to be ashamed of. What happened was my fault." He paused. "You seemed pretty shaken when you ran out."

Sweat beaded along her upper lip and she licked it away. She ran trembling fingers through her hair. She rubbed the tense muscles at the back of her neck. "I'm okay now."

"Honey, I want to see you again. Not for—I mean just to talk. Maybe we could go sailing. You'd be safe on my boat—even with me—because *Enchantress* is sixty feet long and a lot more than I can handle alone. And I don't have a captain. It's cold out there, and we'd be too bundled up in wet gear to touch each other."

Joshua was asking her out again.

Some unwise, traitorous, feminine side of her wanted to forget about Nell, wanted to surrender to the swift, hot urgency in his low, emotion-charged tone.

Fortunately her wiser side primly asserted itself. "I—I don't think that's such a good idea."

"I'm sure you're right," he admitted, but his tightly coiled voice was tinged with dark disappointment.

"I—I was about to call Nell and resign as apartment manager," Honey forced herself to continue briskly.

"So..." That old edge of bitterness that she hated had crept into his voice. "You're giving up on me... Just when you were beginning to make progress."

"Progress?" Honey asked quietly. "What do you mean?"

"No one's ever affected me the way you do."

No one had ever affected her the way he did either.

"That could be bad for both of us."

"Maybe. We'll never know if you move away." He hesitated. "I've been different lately—since you."

The memory of his mouth on her lips and body stirred hotly through her. "In what way?"

"You said you wanted to motivate me to be nicer. Well, maybe you have...just a little. The other day I helped a kid who works for me out of a jam. It felt good." He hesitated. "I'm helping a widow, an old friend, who was broke and alone and in trouble with a kid to support. She's going to sing in one of my hotel clubs till I can figure out what else to do. And yesterday I called my ex-wife and apologized for the way I treated her during our marriage. I told her how much Heather still needs her. She called Heather."

Honey twisted her wedding ring around and around on her finger. "Joshua, I—I really don't see—"

"I've even decided I can live with my view. I'll leave Nell's building and her tenants alone. I'll let you win. That is,

Ms.—I mean *Mrs.*—Rodriguez, if you stay for the summer."

"I thought you didn't want me on your hill?"

"You were right when you said I was conceited to think of it as my hill. I want to share it . . . with you."

A desperate lump rose in Honey's throat. "Why would you back off? You said you never give up when you set out to do something."

"And you said a man could change."

"But have you? Really?"

"If you leave, we'll never know."

"And if I stay—" As she twisted her ring, it came off in her hand.

"I can't promise. All I know is that my priorities are different. I want to please you."

She knew she shouldn't listen, but somewhere inside her hammered the persistent advocate for his defense. "I—I don't know what to say. I feel all mixed up. I guess I can't really believe I've made any real difference to you."

"Oh, but you have. I've been chased by demons for as long I can remember. When I'm with you, they seem a long way behind me. I don't always feel the need to attack everybody like I used to."

"I don't know what to say."

"Just go sailing with me."

She wanted to. Still, she hesitated.

A balmy, all-enveloping coolness was drifting up from the waterfront, stealing up the hill into her open windows. She could almost smell the salty tang of the bay, she could almost feel the freshening wind. Mario's raspy, sensual voice and music drifted inside too.

Now was the time to say no to sailing. To say no to Joshua forever. She tried, but somehow the word stuck in her throat.

Instead it was his name, a whispery velvet invitation laced with sadness and longing, that escaped her lips.

"Joshua—"

He sensed her hunger. It was in his voice, too. "Honey—"

They both laughed nervously, huskily—together.

"I can't seem to say no," she said simply. She opened a drawer and threw her wedding ring inside.

"Good. I'll call you Saturday." Then he hung up.

She set the receiver in its cradle and put her hands to her face. She felt cold and hot at the same time. What had she done? Why couldn't she be smart and let Joshua go?

Because the mere thought was torture. Because without him, her future stretched ahead of her like a bleak and empty wasteland.

She had spent most of her life running from her father's coldness and materialistic cynicism. She had married Mike to prove she was not that kind of person. How could she embrace a man who was even darker than her father, a man who espoused all her father's worst characteristics—who in fact went further than her father with the same stifling, abhorrent views? A man who threatened everything she had always tried to believe in, all her most sacred ideals? A man who would show her no mercy when he found out she was Cecilia Wyatt, when he found out she had deliberately tricked him.

The mainsail was tight and full, but the jib spilled air as *Enchantress* tacked to windward. Normally Joshua would have trimmed the sail. Today he was too distracted by the woman at his side.

Joshua still found it hard to believe Honey had come out with him. He watched the wind and the sunlight play across her eager face and he was filled with pleasure and wonder. She smiled—that special smile that both charmed him and mystified him because it always gave him a curious feeling of familiarity. Yet if he had known her surely by now he would have placed her.

She was a natural sailor. She liked being out on the bay as much as he did. It was odd, but for a working girl, she hadn't seemed impressed with the yacht club or the fancy yachts as his dates usually were.

Honey was leaning against the lifelines, wearing his bright yellow foul-weather gear which swallowed her, not minding as Monica or Simone would have minded that she didn't look fashionable, that the humid wind tangled her hair. When an occasional wave doused her with frigid saltwater, she ducked and laughed.

San Francisco looked beautiful from the water. On one side the hills swept down to the purple Pacific like giant folds of red-gold fleece. On the opposite shore the buildings were tinged with slanting pink light.

The sun was going down and the cold breeze was picking up. As the lavender evening began to darken, so did his mood.

His brown hand spun the wheel all the way to starboard, and he shouted, "Coming about. It's late. We have to go in."

"I wish we could stay out here forever," Honey said wistfully.

When they turned back toward the club, the skyscrapers glowed even redder from their new angle. So did the waves. It looked like they were sailing across fire.

His eyes met hers, and in that unguarded moment he knew she understood that he felt even more reluctant than she to return. He always felt freer on a boat, easier. That's why he'd brought her sailing. He'd wanted to be with her just once without his fierce tensions taking over.

"I had a wonderful time today," she said. A dolphin sprang out of the glistening water, and she laughed. Then she turned and smiled at him.

He knew he had known her before. But where? When?

"There's another one," he shouted.

The long sloop sliced gracefully through the white foaming waves toward the gleaming city.

"When I was a kid, I used to bicycle down to the waterfront and watch the little rich kids getting on boats like this with their parents. I never dreamed I'd own one myself," he said bitterly.

"She's beautiful."

"*Enchantress* is first class. Sixty feet of perfection. She's got a tough, fiberglass hull that cuts through chop like a razor."

"And she's lovely down below. All that polished teak."

"I oil it myself—to relax."

He had already explained how each of the dozens of state-of-the-art, high-tech nautical instruments aided in navigation. Honey hadn't laughed when he'd told her that some day he wanted to sail around the world.

"I'm glad you're a sailor and not a mountain climber," she said.

"Why?"

"Because I'm afraid of heights."

She was looking up at him almost shyly, smiling *that smile*. Was she saying it was important to her to enjoy the things he enjoyed?

"This boat is the only thing I've ever bought that's given me something back. When I sail, I leave all my problems and anger on shore."

She stared at the glistening city, at the fiery skyscrapers, then at him. There was an intensity about her expression as she studied him, an anxious something in her eyes that he'd never seen in other women's, a need for him that was much more than physical. There was fear, as well.

"Maybe you should sail more often." She glanced past him. Her frightened face grew still.

He was filled with guilt. "After the other day," he began hoarsely, "at your school—"

"Don't—" She turned back to him and moved closer, pressing her shaking fingertips to his lips. "I want to enjoy this moment."

So did he. As always her slightest touch made him hot, hotter than he wanted to be. He folded her hand in his, pressed it against his cheek and held it there for a long moment before he let it go. "I wouldn't have blamed you if you hadn't come."

"I wanted to see you again," she said gently, her quivery voice betraying her fear.

"It's probably difficult for someone with your high ideals to understand a man like me."

She stared at him in mute dismay for a long moment. "Like you said—I'm no saint."

"Compared to me—"

"No." She swallowed. "You were closer to the truth before. I'm no angel. I wanted people to think I was."

"A mysterious woman?"

She smiled and shivered, a little nervously, not looking at him, and just for a second he almost believed she really did have something to hide.

He pointed out two buildings he had built, and she complimented them. He showed her the hotel he was renovating. "You can see the new tower going up—to the right of the Transamerica Pyramid."

"It's wonderful. So modern. I'm impressed."

He fought against the sudden warmth her praise brought. "So far, that's all my life has been about—owning, taking. Making money. That's all that mattered." He looked at her, and her soft smile set off every erogenous nerve ending in his body. *Until now. Until you.*

He stopped himself. He didn't want to push her again too fast. "I'd better shut up," he finished awkwardly.

"No, I really do want to know more about you. How did you get the hotel?"

He trimmed the mainsail. "Like I've gotten most things—in an unfriendly takeover." His face darkened. "The same way I'll get that one—over there."

When he pointed toward the Wyatt Hotel, her whole body tensed. Her white fingers went taut on the lifelines.

Joshua scarcely noticed because his fiercest demons were back. He was a little boy again playing with his toy locomotive on that long ago rainy Sunday morning when a violent gunshot had exploded, shattering the silence, the

peace, his life—forever. He had run down the narrow basement stairs only to scream endlessly when he found his
father's lifeless body crumpled over his shotgun and broken whiskey bottle in a pool of blood. Joshua had dropped
the locomotive and run all the way to the church so his
mother would come home and make everything all right
again. He remembered the horrors of the hospital, the funeral—how he'd felt cut off from it all, how his mother
hadn't cared about anything ever again, not even her son.
He remembered how he'd gone up to Hunter Wyatt's gigantic desk only to cower with impotent terror when Wyatt
laughed at him and blurted out the awful truth—that he was
a spineless wimp, just like his father.

Joshua's narrow blue gaze had iced over. "I'm going to
buy the Wyatt chain and sell it off piece by piece until there's
nothing left of Wyatt but the memory of his name."

"You mean another hostile takeover?" Honey asked
faintly.

"Very hostile." All his seething tensions had returned.
"Sometimes I think my whole life's been about that hotel—getting it back, destroying it. But what I really want is
to destroy Wyatt himself."

"Why?" Her low voice was choked, thready. Her tongue
came out and wet her lips.

"Revenge. As a kid, I wanted to kill him. I had to get
some years on me before I realized killing's never any
good—"

"Thank God—" Her eyes were frantic.

His deep voice was glacier cold. "I meant killing's always too easy."

"But why? Why are you so set on this? Have you thought
of his family? His wife? His children?"

"Why should I give a damn about them?"

"Because they're human beings. Because you are too."
She scrambled against the cabin, away from him. "Let
Hunter Wyatt go, Joshua."

"Are you crazy?"

"I'm not asking you to do it for me. Do it for yourself."
Her wide, panicked eyes held incomprehensible misery, and
yet at the same time she stood her ground, challenging his
entire code of living. "Let him go, Joshua. Go forward with
your life."

"You have no idea what you're asking," he yelled before
he remembered he shouldn't blame her.

She was too sweet and gentle, too altruistic to understand how guilt and grief and hatred could twist a person.
He had probably frightened her by revealing his dark am-
bitions so forcefully. But before he could explain why he
could never do as she'd asked, his radar's alarm went off.

Three loud squawks.

He looked under his sail and felt an immediate jolt of
alarm. His pupils dilated. His dark face went white. Honey
screamed.

Hell.

An enormous megayacht, on a collision course with *Enchantress,* was bearing down on their port side.

Joshua was under sail and on a starboard tack which
meant he had the right-of-way on two counts. Not that
right-of-way rules mattered when his hull was about to be
crushed like a matchbox beneath a roaring freight train
which could easily kill them both.

Joshua forgot everything but the deadly, frothing bow
wave crashing toward them. His hand tightened on the
wheel.

"Tacking! Now!" He spun the wheel to starboard and
held it there.

Enchantress careened clumsily into a tall wave and was
stopped dead by the wall of water and strong current. Her
jib backed, and she heeled over. Water and spray broke
across the bow and decks, flooding her cockpit.

The power yacht charged relentlessly toward them. Honey
groped her way forward through the water and struggled to
loosen her jib sheet from the winch and bring the big sail
across.

Just when Joshua thought all was lost and he pulled Honey into his arms to shield her with his own body, the pilot of the other yacht saw them, veered and passed underneath them, missing them in that last split second by no more than a few inches, the huge yacht's churning wake rocking *Enchantress* violently.

Joshua let Honey go and watched the yacht speed recklessly away. *The bastards were either drunk or on something.*

He turned wild, furious eyes on Honey. She could have been chopped to pieces. That thought and how much he cared scared the hell out of him.

"That was close. Too close," he whispered, softening when he saw her fear.

Joshua had completely forgotten Hunter Wyatt. "Those bastards could have killed us, but you were great, the way you handled that sail—a natural," Joshua said, setting the automatic pilot, reaching for her.

She came into his arms, soft and small and seeking his strength like a frightened child. Their heavy foul-weather gear crinkled.

"I was a little scared," she admitted.

He could feel her shaking. Hell, he was shaking, too.

"It's over," he murmured softly. Her wet hair flew against his face, and he brushed it aside. "Nothing like this has ever happened out here to me before, but we're okay." His hand lingered against her cheek before he pulled it away. He was so glad she was safe he wanted to gather her closer and kiss her hard, but he remembered how he'd treated her in her classroom and held back.

"I hope we are—okay," she said, shaking, still afraid, clinging.

"Honey, Honey." His low voice soothed as he framed her face in his palms and drew her even closer. For a long time he held her, until she quieted and he felt his body tighten in a hot male way that told him he'd better let her go.

"So tell me about yourself," Joshua rasped, to distract them both, gently pushing her away.

"What do you want to know?"

"Everything." He made his voice casual. "Start when you were a little girl. I'll bet you were cute."

The wake of another boat caused *Enchantress* to rock. He steadied Honey with his hand.

"I was a brat. I made a terrible childhood even worse than it needed to be."

"You were poor?"

"No. I was rich. Very rich. We had mansions, servants, yachts, cars."

"You were lucky then."

Her eyes were huge. "No. You should know such things don't matter much."

"They do when you don't have them."

"My mother died," she said quietly. "My father remarried. My only brother was deeply disturbed by everything that happened. Instead of helping him, my father drove him away. After that I was alone with my father. When he wasn't ignoring me, he made my life miserable in other ways."

"What was he like?"

Did he only imagine that she flinched? That she was afraid again?

"I—I really don't want to talk about it." But after a while she did. "I was very unhappy after my brother left. I tried to find him, and when I couldn't I went through a rebellious stage. Then I got married—deliberately—to a man my father didn't approve of. After that I was totally estranged from my family. I guess I was fairly happy, until Mike died. And Mario started acting so wild. I tried to find my brother again, but it's like he disappeared off the face of the earth." Her sad voice trailed off.

"What happened then?"

"I kept Mario with me. Maybe because he reminds me of my brother. You see, my father should have taken my brother in hand, but he was too busy making money and trying to make his young wife happy. Nobody but me cared, and I was too young to help him. Sometimes I think I've spent most of my life trying to right the wrongs of my childhood."

"Tell me about it! My life has been a one-man vendetta since my father died."

"Why?"

Joshua tried not to see again the shrunken body of his father on the basement floor, but the vision overpowered him. Suddenly his chest felt tight, constricted, but when he took a deep gulp of air it just got tighter. He remembered the hospital, his father's strange stiff face, the coldness of his father's big hands that had once been so gentle, the dead, lost eyes in his mother's living face. At the funeral Joshua had wished that he could crawl in the coffin and be buried too.

All the dark grief and anger came back like it was yesterday. "It was a long time ago," he muttered bitterly. "It shouldn't matter any more."

"But it does."

"Yeah." His throat worked convulsively. "He was good to me. It still hurts."

"Maybe you should fight harder to let it go," she said in a stricken tone. "He wouldn't have wanted you to grieve forever."

His gaze shifted to touch her animated face—her lovely pale skin, her fiery hair, her big, luminous green eyes. Then her mouth. God, how he longed for the sweetness of it melting against his lips.

She was sweet. No one had ever seemed so sweet, so honest. All his life he'd been starved for the taste and touch of a woman like her. But she didn't understand. How could she? He was afraid to let go of the hate.

A twisted, churning rawness knotted his insides. He leaned forward and touched her face, tilting her chin back. His wayward caress of her silken skin was dangerously comforting to him, dangerously pleasurable. She made him know how lonely he was—how he craved her, only her.

"I'm not very good at letting go of intense feelings," he muttered. "Once they get a grip, they're like acid eating me alive on the inside—till I do something about them."

He shouldn't have touched her again. But now that he had, he couldn't stop.

His hand moved possessively lower to the base of her throat. He felt her pulse wildly fluttering beneath his fingertips. The waves rocked the boat and they fell against each other, their bodies intimately locking as the yacht heeled.

"Joshua, you have to let go of the bad feelings to have the good ones," she said in a hushed voice, holding on to him.

"It's not that easy." His hand, which had become tangled in her flying hair, tensed. "Anyway, I'd rather feel nothing."

"You keep saying you don't want love—" There was a throbbing ache in her voice.

"Because I don't. Love is a hook set deep in your heart that sooner or later rips you to pieces." Before he thought, he grabbed her by the shoulders and pulled her into his body. As always she felt good. So good, his insides curled with pleasure. So good, dark, hot desire throbbed through every male cell.

"Then why did you ask me out?" she whispered.

"Because I want this." His fingers dug into the tender flesh of her shoulders and he eased her closer against the supple strength of his male body.

She drew a deep worried breath. "So, nothing's changed?"

"Why do you want to complicate something that can be good for us both?"

"Joshua, I can't live on hate the way you can," she whispered, lifting a shaking hand so that her fingertips could gently trace the iron line of his jaw.

"Maybe you won't have to very long." He was surprised at the vehemence in his voice.

She seemed to swallow between heartbeats. "Because you only want me for a night or two."

When he didn't deny it, her eyes misted; her hand fell slowly away from his rugged face. "Joshua, if this is your best offer, please, do me a favor. Don't call me—ever again."

His hushed laughter was harsh. "You want me just as much as I want you." His hard hands drew her nearer. "You know you do."

"Yes, but every time you touch me you're setting your hook in me. I don't want to be hurt any more than you do." She tried to shake him off. "If you can't try to feel something for me, let me go, Joshua. Please—"

Take or be taken. His large hands tightened on her waist.

"Oh, Joshua. Are you really so selfish? So brutal? Do you really think you're the only one who's ever been hurt? All my life I've wanted love. I've felt so alone ever since my mother died and my brother ran away."

He'd been alone too. "You were married."

She winced. "I never felt this way about him. And I feel terrible because I couldn't. Mike was so good, so decent—"

"Damn it. The last thing I want to hear about is how unfavorably I compare to your saintly husband!" Joshua's hands were making their way inside her foul-weather-gear jacket. He wanted to crush her against the cabin and smother her with kisses. To kiss her until she begged him to take her.

"Joshua, I don't think I was meant to love a saint. I think I could love you. But if you can't even try to feel something for me, be kind and let me go."

Be kind? He laughed harshly.

Take or be taken. Use or be used. Desire pulsed through him like a volcanic river of fire.

Suddenly he kissed her hard, fusing his hot lips to hers, his mouth and tongue claiming fierce possession.

The yacht rolled down a wave.

"Please, Joshua, let me go."

He didn't want to, but when he looked into her terrified eyes, he realized it wasn't so easy to apply his old code of

living any more. How could he take her or use her—when
he knew she would never do those things to him?

Somehow, inexplicably, her softness had softened the hate
in him. He remembered how he'd nearly made love to her on
her classroom floor and had forced himself to stop.

As his grip slackened, she wrenched herself free and
scurried down below into the cabin as though she were truly
terrified of him now. She slammed the hatch shut, leaving
him in the cockpit to sail the rest of the way to the marina
alone.

Damn. Was he a monster? Or was he just as scared as she
was? If she took away the hate, what the hell would he have
left?

The velvet, icy darkness seemed to swallow him. He
turned on the running lights. The night grew colder, so cold
that Joshua felt chilled all the way to the marrow of his
bones.

Eleven

Two weeks. Honey had lived two weeks without him.
Without his touch and with the terrible feeling that her heart
was encased in ice. But somehow she had managed to go on,
even though she'd thought of Joshua almost constantly.

Today had been especially bad until Mario had accidentally let Emerald escape and she'd been so preoccupied trying to catch her bird that she couldn't think of anything else.
Thus, Joshua was not on her mind as Honey pried the thick
leaves apart and peered through them.

Emerald was sitting high up in the apple tree, smug as
could be, munching calmly. He had been there five hours
and was in no mood to leave. Honey was frantic to catch
him before it got dark, but as she nudged the ladder against
the thin trunk which grew precariously close to the edge of
the cliff, she heard the whir of traffic a hundred feet below.

She had assembled her parrot-catching kit too hastily. It
consisted of Emerald's cage, her green bedspread and a pair
of gloves. Unfortunately, she hadn't been able to find her
net—a crucial item. So, she would have to climb.

When she put a foot on the bottom rung, the whole tree shook. Rocks tumbled down the sheer wall of the cliff. Emerald squawked and jumped to a higher limb. The ladder wobbled as she climbed to the second rung.

She looked down—all the way down—to the pavement and cars below. Bits of apple plunked onto her head. When her foot missed the third rung, her heart fluttered. Another bit of apple bounced off the tip of her nose. Emerald was probably taking deliberate aim. The higher she climbed, the louder Emerald squawked and the dizzier she felt.

Mario saw her predicament and jumped up, leaving Tina on the porch, to come over to help. He was instantly bombed by apple bits. "I bet next time you won't put off clipping his wings."

All Honey's frustrations zeroed in on Mario. "The last thing I need from you right now, young man, is advice. You shouldn't have left the door open while I was trying to collect Mrs. Conklin's rent."

He shot her a dazzling smile. "Sorry, but when Tina came by I forgot."

More apple whizzed past them, hurtling all the way down the cliff, splattering onto the street.

"Why don't you make yourself useful and hold—"

Mario was about to brace the ladder, when the phone rang.

"It's probably one of your girlfriends," she hissed.

He smiled. "Hang on. I'd better answer it—so Tina won't."

"Mario, she'll call back—"

But he was already gone. She looked down at the cars again and got dizzy.

He returned a minute later. "It's for you."

Honey crawled down the ladder and took the cordless phone.

"Cecilia, darling—"

"Astella—"

"I hope I didn't take you away from anything important."

More chunks of apple rained down.

"My parrot got loose."

"Guess who called? J. K. Cameron—with an offer to sell us all his Wyatt stock over the next few months—at a low price we'll be able to afford."

"Joshua? I don't understand. I begged him to do that two weeks ago, but he refused."

"Well, something must have changed his mind." Astella's voice was cool. "Maybe you did."

Honey could feel her heart beginning to thump with excitement. *Had he done it for her?*

"Cecilia, we've won. You can move home. I think your father is grateful even though he's not about to admit it. However, he did say he wants you away from Cameron—at once. Mario can come, too."

"What if Joshua changes his mind again?"

"The only thing that might make him do that is if he finds out about you. You've got to back off, Cecilia. Fast. If you stay, you jeopardize everything."

Leave Joshua? When he might be starting to care?

Quite suddenly all her happiness vanished. "You're right, I suppose." Her voice was soft and sad.

"You should be thrilled! We won! I think your father is even on the verge of forgiving us for interfering."

"Thrilled . . ." Honey's low tone was muffled as she said goodbye.

Joshua's five-story house cast a long shadow over her house. She looked up at his bedroom window. His blinds were drawn. She would never see him again. She felt bleak, empty.

She had won. She had everything she had wanted and more. Why then did she feel so cold that she had begun to shiver, so cold that she was afraid something vital and fragile had died inside her forever?

From the hill above she heard a sound. A tall man with a lithe, muscular body was descending the Filbert Steps with the easy, silent grace of a large predatory cat.

Joshua. She tensed expectantly as she remembered that first day when she'd been so terrified after she'd left him that note. He'd come down those same steps toward her. He had kissed her and her lips had burned for hours afterward.

Joshua stepped into the open, looking darker and more dangerous than ever. He wore black slacks and a black silk shirt that showed his lean, powerful build.

Their eyes met and held across the late afternoon shadows.

The wind blew his black hair across his tanned brow. In his eyes she saw profound emotion.

Her heart gave a leap of pure happiness. She gasped, clutching the ladder because she wanted to fly toward him, into his arms.

No, she didn't have everything she wanted.

Not any more.

Now she wanted a cold, dark man who didn't know how to love and didn't want to learn. She wanted a man who'd spent his life living for revenge, a man who was everything she wanted to run from—the one man her father hated more than all others.

Her father had forgiven her Mike. He would never forgive her Joshua.

But as she stared into the dazzling warmth of Joshua's blue eyes, it didn't matter.

Nothing mattered except Joshua.

"Looks like you could use some help," Joshua murmured in an odd voice. "I brought a net."

"Hey, that's great," she answered weakly, feeling heady with delirium and shy too.

Mario moved back to the porch. Heather, who had followed her father, joined Tina and him there.

Joshua came up to Honey. His gaze roamed her shapely body. "God, how I missed you."

Never had such simple words been filled with more erotic longing.

Her warm green eyes sparkled. Then she felt shy again.

"Don't you know it's not safe to look at me like that," he muttered, his cynical voice slightly hoarse, even as her adoring eyes stayed fastened on him defiantly.

"Oh, Joshua," she moaned helplessly. "I thought I wanted you to stay away and leave me alone."

"I know." His eyes were hot as hers; his voice was tender. "It's hell with you. It's hell without you, too. I don't know who I am or what I want. Everything that used to matter doesn't matter any more."

She held the ladder for him while he climbed the tree and caught her parrot.

Three passing tourists descending the Filbert Steps applauded when his net snagged Emerald just as the parrot was spreading his wings to take off for a towering pine. The teenagers on the porch laughed as Emerald squawked and jumped furiously in the net as he was brought down and carried inside.

Honey shut the door and opened the net, and Emerald flew to his perch and stared out at the apple tree sulkily.

She turned to Joshua and was struck by the force of his bronzed virility and his startling blue eyes. "I owe you. How can I repay you?" she asked, feeling a little faint.

"I think you know." His voice was a husky caress tingling down her spine. "By giving me another chance."

Radiant confusion colored her face as she turned away.

"You have all the rare qualities I never knew I wanted in a woman. You're sweetly loving, honest—"

The color drained from her face. "Joshua, there's something I'd better tell you."

He caught her to him. His fingers smoothed the worry lines between her brows. "Don't. No problems now. We can always talk. I'd rather not spoil the mood. We've both waited for this—too long."

He was right. The sweetness of their new beginning was too fragile. So, she opened her lips as his sensual mouth moved tantalizingly nearer and let him kiss her in that wild, hungry way that made her want much more.

* * *

The hotel bar was bathed in candlelight as Honey stepped out of the elevator on Joshua's arm. She wore a sleek green silk gown. Her red hair fell against her pale neck in a satiny pageboy. Her cheeks were aglow. She knew that tonight would be a night she would want to remember always.

Later. After they had tonight, there would be a right moment to tell him who she really was.

Then she saw the tall, dark man with the distinctive spray of silver in his jet black hair and the warm, surprised, cat-stole-the-cream grin that came over his face the instant he saw her. Honey froze as Johnny Midnight made his way toward them, thick legal papers stuffed into one dark hand, a scotch and soda in the other.

Midnight looked at her wrists and grinned knowingly when she blushed at the humiliating memory of their first meeting. "Now this is a surprise." Midnight turned to J.K. "Sorry I'm late with these. Look them over before your meeting with Mrs. Wyatt."

Honey stared at both men, her heart thumping, her mind paralyzed.

"Thanks, Midnight. I'll call you tomorrow, before the meeting."

Midnight didn't leave. Instead his smile warmed. "Aren't you going to introduce me to the lady?"

Honey felt doomed as Joshua's possessive arm moved her forward. "Honey Rodriguez, Johnny Midnight, my lawyer."

"My pleasure, *Miss Rodriguez,*" Midnight said smoothly as he folded her icy, shaking hand in his warm one. When she tried to pull away, he held it a second longer than he should have. "You must be J.K.'s new *neighbor.*"

"She's off limits, Midnight. She's very special to me."

Midnight shrugged, "So I see. You two look good together. Hey, why don't you both join me for a quick drink?"

No. No. No. Terrified, Honey stared numbly into Midnight's determined dark eyes.

Joshua shrugged. "Why not? If that's okay with you, Honey?"

Honey swallowed, miserable, and nodded mutely, not looking at him.

Midnight stared straight at her. "Joshua's been different—since you."

She sucked in a quick, sharp breath. "Oh?"

When she nearly tripped as she followed both men to the table, Midnight rushed to help her regain her balance. She was so flustered she let him seat her beside the window without even noticing the fifty-story drop. Then she looked down, and grabbed onto Joshua's arm. His hand closed over hers so protectively that she almost felt safe. Till she saw Midnight absorbing the tender moment.

Midnight paid for the first round. Honey gulped her white wine frantically while the two men talked.

All too soon Midnight turned to her, pretending no more than polite interest. "When J.K. told me he had a new girlfriend, I never expected it to be you—I mean someone like you."

Honey spluttered something inaudible as she choked on her wine.

Joshua patted her back and said smoothly, "She's a refreshing change."

The centerpiece of their table was composed of golden roses nestled around a single candle. Honey reached nervously for a rose and knocked over the burning candle. Midnight grabbed it just in time.

"Careful. It's always dangerous to play with fire," came Midnight's knife-edged, satin drawl. He eyed her steadily and blew out the flame.

Joshua's hand closed over hers. "Midnight, it took forever to get her to trust me enough to date me. Don't scare her away."

Midnight got up. "That was never my intention."

"She's in no danger from me."

"Maybe from herself then."

Midnight's soft words terrified Honey. Any minute Joshua was going to sense Midnight's not-so-hidden agenda.

Instead Joshua got angry. "What the hell are you driving at?"

Midnight ignored Joshua and leaned toward Honey. "He's one dangerous guy. Play it straight."

She was too terrified to speak; Joshua was too furious. In the confusion Midnight relit their candle and made a swift exit.

Joshua's arm circled her shoulders protectively. "What the hell was that all about?" A dark, angry note lingered in his low tone. "You two know each other?"

"No..." As Honey looked across the golden glow of their candle into Joshua's swarthy face, she felt thoroughly shaken. But she couldn't tell Joshua, not yet.

The band began to play—soft, romantic music.

"Do you want to dance?" Joshua asked, as if he was as ill at ease as she was.

The candlelight made her eyes sparkle like fiery, dark emeralds. "Oh, yes." Anything to forget Midnight's dark warning.

When he wrapped her in his arms, she felt the heat of his body and the hardness of his muscles. She laid her head over his violently thudding heart. Soon she was floating in a dream as he swirled her on the dance floor.

Other dancers twirled past them in a blur. After a while they were alone, dancing in the darkness near the sheer glass windows with the city and the bridges and the hills sparkling beneath them. She was breathless. Not from the height, but from being in Joshua's arms. His hot mouth found her silken nape, and she felt an electric quickening radiate every time his lips nuzzled her skin.

The hours passed like minutes and all too soon the candle at the center of their table had melted to a nub, its flame glimmering darkly from its crystal saucer. And still they danced, their bodies swaying rhythmically, aware only of their escalating need.

At one point Joshua led her away from the bar into a dark corner. She looked down—fifty stories down—and then breathlessly into Joshua's eyes. He took her fingers in his and brought them slowly to his lips. She felt his calluses and was reminded of his brutality even as the warmth of his lips caressed her fingertips.

The flickering candlelight accentuated the unrelenting harshness of his carved face.

Suddenly she was terrified. Could a man really change when he'd lived as roughly as Joshua had?

"You're afraid—of me?" he whispered, letting her go.

She struggled to smile. "I don't want to be."

His gaze fastened on her lips. He drew a deep breath. "Do you know," he began, "that sometimes I have the strangest feeling we've met before. I felt it the first time I met you— when you smiled."

She looked out the window and began to tremble violently. "Perhaps in another life—"

"No! This life."

His handsome, dark face was dangerously near hers; his vitality vibrated across her nerve endings, making her sharply, dangerously aware of him. And dangerously aware of her lie.

"I could never have forgotten you, Joshua." The half truth burned her lips and her conscience. "Never."

"I could never have forgotten you, either. That what's so damn puzzling." He lifted her chin, tilting her pale face to his. "Don't worry, one of these days it'll hit me," he whispered as his mouth descended toward hers. "Just like that!" When he snapped his fingers she jumped away from him.

"Hey, there's no reason to be afraid." He took her tremulous lips in another slow, hot kiss. It was as if he instinctively sought to erase her terror and guilt with melting passion, to make her know that he was a lonely man who craved her as no other man ever had.

She shivered, more afraid than ever by the completeness of her intimate longing for him. There was no way she could let him go. No way. No matter what it cost her.

Her hands circled his neck and clung. She wanted to be with him, tonight—forever.

When he felt the shuddering upheaval of her breasts that betrayed her inner torment, he pulled his mouth from hers. With a hot hand he brushed her cheek. "Let's get the hell out of here."

Careful not to touch, hardly daring to look at each other, they stepped into the elevator just as a beautiful woman with long golden hair began to sing from the stage. Her husky, smoky voice had a hauntingly lovely velvet sound.

"She's good," Honey said as the bronze doors closed, seeking what she thought was a safe neutral subject.

"She's Lacy Doug—Lacy Miller, an old friend, fallen onto hard times, dangerous times," Joshua said harshly. "She's not a professional singer, but she's good enough to be one. I'd introduce you to her some time, but I'm arranging for her to leave the country. Midnight was in love with her once."

"And?"

Joshua's expression darkened. "Same old story. She left him for a richer man. He was Johnny's former...boss. Lacy knew Johnny had grown to distrust and detest Douglas, and she still betrayed Johnny to him anyway."

"How?"

"She lied," he murmured, the old bitterness in his voice. "And now he hates her. Douglas was murdered, the assets of her husband's estate have been frozen, and she thinks Douglas's killer is after her. She's running for her life, and I'm trying to help her—a fact I don't dare tell Midnight since he's so inflexible once he makes up his mind."

Something in his dark, derisive look terrified her. "A-and was her lie...so terrible?"

"Midnight thought so," he muttered in a violent undertone. "That's what counts, isn't it?"

Joshua's eyes and voice were so coldly piercing that her secret breathless hope died. She cowered from him in the darkest corner of the elevator, so he wouldn't read her guilt and suspect that she too was a liar.

Tell him.

But his face had been ravaged by the unhappy memory, or by some loneliness all his own.

Her body felt icy, all its heat gone. She fought against her rising panic.

He sensed her distress and drew her into his arms and kissed her violently, demandingly. "There's so much I want to forget," he muttered in a low, tortured tone. "So many demons from the past that haunt me." His mouth descended once more in a long kiss that left her breathless.

Her hand went up, wavered, and then curved timidly around his neck to hold him closer. "I love you," she whispered.

A little bell went off and the elevator stopped at a floor. Reluctantly they drew apart before the doors opened.

No one was there. The doors closed.

Joshua drew her against himself and ran his hand across her smooth cheek. His fingers ruffled through her hair. He looked at her with eyes that hungered for more than her body, with a need that seemed to shake him. But he couldn't speak. He could only lower his mouth and search for the rapid pulse beating at her throat.

His lips were so gentle and hot they made her sigh. His pain was her pain because she loved him, and it thrilled her that he sought comfort in her arms.

Dear God, she had to tell him the truth. But as his mouth moved to her lips again and his kisses deepened, she didn't know how she could.

Twelve

Joshua's powerful sports car roared up and down through the sparkling hills. He was driving fast, dangerously fast, and yet with consummate skill. He downshifted, his headlights arcing off the walls of closely stacked Victorian houses as he whipped around a sharp turn, his tires shrilling as they burned the pavement. He frowned at the narrow street ahead lined with parked cars, his eyes concentrating on the flying dark. Honey felt his wildness, his willingness to embrace danger, and she gloried in it because the same volatile aphrodisiac pulsed in her blood.

The rush of cool wind and the moonlight was in her hair. His hard, possessive arm tightened around her shoulders as the car made the final climb up to Telegraph Hill. She felt an almost physical pain deep in her belly.

He made her feel wild—wild enough to stand on the edge of the highest precipice and take a flying leap over the side.

The car snarled up the hill. When he swerved to an abrupt stop in his darkened garage, he cut the engine and pulled her close, gripping her fiercely against his body.

Then he pushed her against the back of her leather seat, his body pressing into hers as he kissed her so hard she couldn't breathe. His large brown hand tunneled through her tangled hair, smoothing it back against her neck. Callused palms shaped her face, traced the slender length of her nose, her lips, her throat, and then trailed over her breasts. His heated lips followed the path of his hands, and she returned his kisses with fevered ones of her own.

"Heather's gone to her mother's," he had said huskily on the drive home.

The garage door rolled down noisily, sealing them into that vast tomb of silent, velvet blackness. At last they were alone—cut off for the rest of the night and from the rest of the world. His shaking hands slid down her body, undoing the buttons at the back of her gown, the rhinestone clasp at her shoulder, yanking her bodice halfway down. As he molded her to him, he was breathing fast and hard. She felt an urgency in him that she had never known before, and the same all-consuming madness was in her as well.

His voice was low and hoarse. "Let's go upstairs."

She could not speak. She did not want to. When he let her go the imprints from his fingers burned her skin, and she had to hold her clothes on as she got out of the car.

She grabbed his tie and pulled him back. Her hands slid inside his waistband and tugged out his shirt, so that her fingertips could explore him, first his muscular back and chest and then lower. His soft laughter was urgent when, at last, she let him go.

Inside his house, she grabbed him again as he unset his burglar alarm. Her hands moved under his clothes, across rippling muscles, bristly chest hair and warm, bare skin. His breath caught as hot, splayed fingertips trailed down his body. He had to key in the numbers twice, to get the code right.

From the bottom story, his spiral staircase wound up five stories to his bedroom. She looked up shakily into the blaze of moonlight that poured through his domed skylight at the top.

Silvery light and shadow distorted the modern paintings that hung against the soaring circular walls. Weird, frightening faces loomed warningly out of the canvases. And she was afraid.

He was Joshua K. Cameron, her father's enemy. *Her enemy.* This was madness. But stronger than her fear of him was her need to be with him.

His intense eyes were on her still white face.

"You're house is so huge," she said. "I feel...sort of funny, like I'm lost."

"It's always been a lonely hell," he murmured. "Until tonight. Until you."

"I've been lonely too, Joshua. Longer than you'll ever know."

Something smoldered dangerously in his eyes. "Now you've got me." Then he pulled her into his arms and she opened her lips to receive his reckless kiss, his searching tongue. A long time later he whispered, "My bedroom is on the fifth floor. I have an elevator."

Her arms slid around his neck. Her hands moved over his broad shoulders, down his muscular torso to tug at his belt buckle. "I'm having fun out here."

His hard mouth touched hers again, this time softly. But it was as if he had set off a fire storm. "Joshua, you're the last man on earth I should feel like this about, the very last man."

"I feel the same way about you." But he kissed her as if he were starving for the taste of her mouth even though he had tasted it only seconds before. She answered his ravening hunger with a need as intense as his.

Her eager hands moved back from his loosened belt to the lapels of his coat, and when she pulled he shrugged out of it. She dropped his coat heedlessly on the stairs and ran past him, up to the second-floor landing where she pretended to admire the magnificent sculpture of a naked woman.

"She's very beautiful," Honey said.

His raspy voice teased from behind her. "Indeed she is."

He caught her to him again, spun her around and placed her against the railing, kissing her again, hard, harder than before. "Very beautiful. And hot. I've never known a woman so hot."

She felt the nothingness falling away behind her and was terrified. The railing seemed deceptively fragile. But his strong arms held her tightly, and more than terror she felt passion as he opened the last of the buttons at the back of her gown. His warm hand moved against her naked back, around her waist, up across her breasts. Then he tugged at her soft dress, and the silk folds slid weightlessly down the length of her voluptuous body. He arched her away from the railing and let her go.

She was wearing a backless green satin slip that clung in all the right places. When his eyes raked her, she laughed a little breathlessly, leaned down and removed each green high heel, one by one and tossed them at him before she raced up four more flights.

He was right behind her, panting hard when they reached the top. She leaned over the edge and gasped at the dizzying drop to the terrazzo floor. He dangled her glittering shoes over the railing before dropping them, and she watched them fall—down, down, like shooting stars until they were lost in the darkness. Her hair swung loosely against her white throat. She turned her wild gaze toward him.

"I thought you were afraid of heights," he murmured.

She stared defiantly into his eyes. "I've decided to live dangerously." She nipped at his mouth wantonly with eager lips. "It's more fun."

His voice was almost gruff. "Not always."

"You would know."

He touched her smooth spaghetti straps and lowered them over her creamy shoulders. "I don't want to hurt you."

But you probably will—maybe you'll even destroy me. She glanced down into the spiraling darkness and then into his dark face. Tonight it was her mood to defy fate. All that mattered was the blazing desire she felt for him.

He was a man shut off from love, from everything bright and safe and truly glorious in the world. A man who took, a man who used. He was everything she'd always run from. And yet she felt his loneliness as if it were her own.

He saw her doubt and her fear; her desire and her defiance. His lips curved into a bitter smile. He would have edged away, but the fierce, lonely need in his eyes drew her like a beacon. Even his terrifying darkness drew her.

She rushed into his arms, and when her body melted into his and she laid her head longingly against his chest she felt him go rock hard. When her shaking fingertips reached up and lovingly traced the rough-edged features of his carved face, he drew a ragged breath.

For a long moment he stood statue still.

Then, very gently he tipped her chin so that he could look into her eyes. They were frightened and yet they sparkled defiantly with passionate fire. He saw her doubt, but he saw her tenderness too.

There was an intensity in his long silence that sent shivers down her spine.

Her fingers loosened the knot of his silk tie. Without a word they began stripping off the rest of their clothes. When they were naked, they lay down on the Aubusson carpet by the stairs, as he covered her with his immense, muscled body, his heat burning her, his mouth devouring her.

She moaned when his hands found her breasts, when his lips greedily raced over her body, sucking her nipples, kissing her everywhere until she felt as torridly on fire as he was.

Even before he thrust wildly inside her, he had swept her away on a burning dark tide, and she knew a total, bewildering oneness with this hard, bitter man that was unlike anything she'd ever felt before—a shattering loss of self that was almost like dying and yet was nothing like dying.

In the white fire of his passion she was reborn.

Until this night, until him, she had never known who she was or what she wanted.

Now she knew.

She knew as well that nothing would ever matter to her more than Joshua.

When the final explosion came, it shook her to the core. Her arms wrapped around his neck and she arched her body into his, pressing her lips into his chest to muffle her scream.

Afterward when she began to cry soundlessly he held her close, and she lay in that tender, silvery darkness against his hard body, which was moist with perspiration, and wondered if he had been as shaken as she.

If he was, he didn't say so. He held her tightly and stared broodingly up at the skylight as though he were studying the moonlight. She reminded herself that he was a man who had had many women—women far more desirable than she, women who would demand far less, women who were not the daughter of his hated enemy.

Joshua was hard and bitter. She was probably a fool to dream that she could change him, a fool to dream that her love was enough to soften him. He would probably hate her when he found out who she was.

But she had wanted tonight even if it was all she could ever have. And even though she would never be sorry, now that it was over all her old terrors were creeping into ascendancy and she was more terrified of him than ever.

When he fell asleep, she lay beside him for a long time. It was nearly morning when she arose and gently covered him with a blanket.

She got dressed slowly and walked sadly down the stairs because she knew that when he found out who she was, she would be the last person on earth he would ever willingly love.

Joshua knew that he wanted the huge emerald the minute he saw it sparkling against black velvet in the jewelry store window. Because it exactly matched *her* eyes.

"How much?" he demanded from the saleslady who showed it to him.

When she named an outrageous figure, he didn't bat an eyelash.

He just pulled out his credit card and handed it to her.
He'd been in a hurry to get to the Wyatt meeting when he'd
seen the ring and known that it didn't matter if the stop
made him late. He had to have it.

Usually he bought jewelry to say goodbye.

But this was different.

Because the woman he was buying it for was so different.

The memory of her erotic sweetness last night, of the way
she had felt when he'd been inside her, made him ache for
her. He didn't understand the power Honey Rodriguez had
over him. All he knew was that he could not live without
her.

Always before, sex had been something he had been able
to keep in perspective. It was an appetite to be satisfied when
he was hungry. There had been great pleasure, and he had
spent a lot of time seeking that pleasure. But there had never
been one woman he had had to have.

That was before *her*.

Last night her wildness and the totality of his own emo-
tional response to her had caught him by surprise. There had
been more of him involved than his body.

The hate was gone from his heart, and a new feeling that
was even more powerful consumed him. He could not name
it.

All he knew was that he was going to ask Honey to marry
him.

The engagement ring was in Joshua's pocket as he strode
toward the Wyatt Hotel with the legal documents Midnight
had given him. There were several details he needed to work
out with Astella Wyatt before he was willing to agree to sell
out to her.

He paused on the steps that led up to the glass doors of
the huge hotel. A dozen red banners with the Wyatt insig-
nia waved from flagpoles. He couldn't bring himself to look
up at the hated flags which would continue to fly over the
hotel that had once been his father's pride and joy. He re-

membered visiting his father in his office here. He had been treated like a crown prince.

Most of all Joshua remembered Wyatt buying out his father, destroying his father, his mother, his own life. He remembered the long years when he had lived with one dream—revenge.

That was the past. Today, because of her, the past had lost some of its terrible power.

Something had happened to him. He wasn't sure what. He only knew that he valued the new feeling in his heart more than the hate, that pleasing Honey mattered more than revenge. He only knew that all the old, dark feelings stood in the way of his new life.

Maybe his wounds were scarring over. Maybe in time the demons' howlings would seem like distant whispers.

Honey had asked him to let Hunter Wyatt go.

Joshua was about to go inside the hotel, when he saw a huge chartreuse car jammed crookedly into a tiny parking space several yards in down the street.

The Bomb.

Her car.

He went back down the steps and smiled at the crazy way she had parked. Honey must be somewhere nearby.

He forgot his meeting and loped toward the Bomb.

As always it was unlocked and untidily crammed with too much junk. He would probably have to hire two maids when he married her and follow her around locking doors and setting alarms. But he smiled when he saw several chocolate-candy wrappers on the front seat and a used book she'd bought, *Why You Never Have to Lose Those Last Ten Pounds*.

The meter had run out. As he dug for a couple of quarters he scanned the street and sidewalk, but she was nowhere in sight.

He plunked both quarters into the meter. When he got done with Astella Wyatt, he would come out and wait till Honey came back because he couldn't wait to ask her to marry him.

But when he returned to the hotel, Honey was coming down the steps. She stopped breathlessly on the third step, looking pale and a little scared.

He wondered why.

Then a red banner flapped, and she tilted her sunglasses up and smiled at him in that special way that always warmed him through.

Only today it rocked him like the coldest wave.

Because at last he knew why her smile had haunted him. Because at last he knew who she really was.

In his mind's eye he saw a blurred vision of a woman in white, of chocolate-candy wrappers, of her warm smile. Most of all he remembered her touch.

She was Cecilia Wyatt from the hospital.

It was all so obvious; why hadn't he seen it before?

Honey reached for him, and he backed away, his stomach tightening sickeningly. One frightened glance into his blazing eyes, and her outstretched hand seemed to freeze in midair.

God, she'd known who he was from the first. She'd sensed that she had some unique power over him even on that first day, that she could turn him soft, and she'd used it. So she'd made herself more attractive, gotten close to him and deliberately ensnared him.

Everything she'd done, everything she'd said was a setup—a lie. Like a fool he'd fallen in love with her.

He grabbed her by the arm and hurried her down the steps.

"Joshua, what's wrong?"

They were both panting when he positioned her against the stone wall of her father's elegant hotel. "You want to know what's wrong? You tell me—*Cecilia!*"

She closed her eyes in mute defense. Then her face tightened as if against some terrible pain, but the rage inside him built. She'd used her sweetness to enchant him, to change him, and all the time she'd been a lying cheat.

Use or be used. She had warned him she'd come after him. She was better at his game than he was. "You were good! Damned good! Your performance last night was the best of all! No wonder you ran out. I'll bet you laughed yourself to sleep last night."

Red Wyatt banners whipped above them, making her still face go light and dark.

Scalding tears slipped from her eyes. "No. I love you, Joshua. I really do!"

"Don't!"

Did she know how her tears and desperately spoken lies tore at his heart? How he would have given everything he owned for them to be the truth? Because now that he knew who she really was, now that he knew she was lost to him, he knew that her love was the only thing he had ever really wanted.

If he despised her, he despised himself more. "You're just saying that for the same reason you've done everything else—to get what you want. I was a fool to think you were different."

She took off her sunglasses. Her tear-filled green eyes were so huge and stricken he would have winced if he hadn't known she was just playing a part.

He grabbed her shaking hand and forced Midnight's legal papers between her clenched fingers. "You tell the people you work for the deal's off." Then he reached into his pocket and pulled out a tiny black velvet box. "Here's something else. I always give the women I sleep with a parting present when I tell them goodbye." His fierce face grew even darker, his savage voice colder. "I spent more than usual, but never mind. Enjoy it. You earned it—*Honey.*"

All the blood drained from her face. The scarlet banners whipped again and held her face in shadow, causing the light to go out of her desperate eyes.

She swayed toward him. Afraid she would faint, he reached for her.

His hand touched hers and she held on to him for a long moment, trembling. He tensed at her touch, hating himself because he liked it, because he craved it. Only when she managed to steady herself, could he relax. Her hand fell away. As he drew back he saw that a single tear traced down her white cheek.

His hard gaze fastened on the sparkling tear. She was good. She was the best. She'd used him. She'd destroyed him. And he was such a wretch he still wanted her.

"Joshua, no... You're wrong. Please, you mustn't believe that I— Last night I wanted to tell you the truth, but I was afraid to tell you. Let me explain."

"I don't give a damn for your lies. I'm going to destroy your father." Joshua's voice softened to a hiss. "But know this—the person I really want to destroy is you."

He turned on his heel and was gone.

"Joshua, please..." Her voice seemed to chase after him—desperate, tear choked.

When she called his name again with a longing that bordered on pain, the husky sound tore his heart like a hook set deeply in soft tissue that was savagely ripped out.

The hardest thing he had ever done was to keep walking away from her.

Thirteen

—

A black flame burned Joshua's soul. He'd thought he'd been in hell before. But this time it was worse. All his demons roamed at will.

He hadn't shaved in two days. He hadn't worked. All he'd done was drink.

Not that whiskey ever helped. Joshua had learned that lesson a long time ago the hard way from his father. Joshua had always known he had his father's weakness. Today was no different. The liquor only made the terrible hatred and the pain and the self-loathing burn all the more fiercely.

He wanted to hate Honey. No. *Cecilia!* He wanted to hate himself, so he'd started the morning off by hitting the bottle especially hard. But the bottle had only made him want her more. For some reason Midnight had chosen today to come by to check on him around noon, when the alcoholic haze had been particularly thick and his hateful desire for her particularly acute. Joshua had greeted Midnight with the order to use every means in his power to destroy the Wyatts and Cecilia.

Midnight had yanked his bottle out of his hand, gone to his bathroom and poured his whiskey down his bathtub drain, yelling, "Hell, no! I won't hurt her *because* you love her, you crazy self-destructive bastard."

Joshua had gone to his bar and opened another bottle. "Then you're fired."

"Oh, no. You can't fire me!" Midnight picked up his leather jacket in disgust. "Because I quit. I'm not going to stick around and watch you rot up here like a street wino instead of trying to understand that she only did what she did because she *had* to. She came to our offices a dozen times to talk to us—no tricks. You called the police. She took you on because you were going to destroy her family."

"If you're so smart about my love life, why are you too damned stubborn to do something about your own? You still love Lacy, but now that Douglas is dead, the guy that killed him—probably Cole Douglas—is after her and her kid. Douglas's assets are frozen and I'm the one who's helping her, who's gotten her fake passports and tickets to Brazil—"

Midnight went sheet white. "Damn you. Who do you think you are—meddling in Lacy's life behind my back? After what she did, she's getting what she deserved from Douglas."

"Does she deserve to die?"

"You stay away from Lacy!"

"You're wrong about her."

"No, I was wrong about you."

Joshua froze at the inflexible rage in his friend's voice. The two men glared at one another with cold mutual dislike, each feeling he'd been stabbed in the back by the other. Only when Midnight slung his coat over his shoulder and raced out of the house, did Joshua's brain clear enough for him to see that he had started their inane quarrel. But when he tried to run down the stairs to stop him, the liquor made him stumble. He fell clumsily against his front door just as Midnight sped away in his latest fast red car.

Joshua felt a terrible guilt about their quarrel, a terrible premonition. He called Midnight's office, but he wasn't there. Nor was he at home.

Joshua's darkness got darker. Without Midnight he was completely alone. And an odd fear took root in the back of his mind and grew.

Joshua stood at his bedroom window and took a pull straight from the bottle. The house was as cold and gray and as hellishly empty as his soul. Since it was no place for a child, he'd ordered Heather move in with Monica for a while, maybe for the rest of the summer.

He stared out the window at Honey's house. She was the cause of everything, even the loss of his daughter and the quarrel with Midnight. Why the hell didn't she go on and move? Was she going to stay down there forever just to torment him?

He took another pull from the bottle. Then he heard his doorbell.

He ignored it. His answering machine was taking all his phone calls.

Whoever was down there pounded defiantly at a window. His doorbell rang again.

It was probably Midnight—determined to resume his defense of Cecilia Wyatt.

Hell. Now that his friend was back Joshua was afraid to see him, because in his present dark mood he would probably just make Midnight more angry. Tomorrow was soon enough to stop drinking and deal with Midnight.

Joshua went to his stereo and turned the music up, so he couldn't hear the pounding and the doorbell.

He jumped when a rock exploded through a glass windowpane and his burglar alarm went off. Shirtless and in old jeans, he staggered out to the landing like a huge, dark, tormented animal.

Honey was standing in the center of his foyer with a scratched wrist and a jagged piece of glass in her hand, looking up at him. As always she wore green.

Her voice was low and frightened, yet he heard it over the pounding stereo.

"Turn off your alarm, Joshua. It's only me."

"The hell I will. I'll let the police come and deal with you for breaking and entering."

"Handcuffs again? I don't think so." She punched in the code herself.

He leaned over the railing. "How the hell did you do that?"

"I watched you."

"Go to hell," he snarled.

She smiled *that* smile, the smile that so haunted him.

"Hey, no need to travel. I'm already there." She came up the stairs slowly, as if she dreaded reaching him as much as he dreaded her.

She was thinner, too skinny for her. How could anyone look so different after a week. Her face was gray; there were dark circles beneath her lifeless eyes. Her red hair didn't shine so much. Her getup was crazy, mismatched. The odd-looking gold bangles at her wrists and ears were cheap and ill chosen. He hated her flowered blouse. She looked like a gypsy, but somehow a very sexy gypsy.

"You look like hell," he muttered darkly. "What do you want?"

"Joshua, I came here because you said it was me you really wanted to destroy—not my father."

He laughed harshly. "Ever the sacrificial lamb."

"You once said you wanted me for a night or two—no complications. Well, you can have me, if you'll just let him go."

His hard gaze raked her body insolently. "I had you—remember? That makes you used merchandise. You don't look so good now. What makes you think I still want you?"

She lowered her lashes against his savage, burning look. But not before he saw that she was trembling, terrified of him.

"Because I can feel it, Joshua. I know you still want me."

He watched the way soft cotton flowers clung to her breasts, the way her skirt swayed against her hips when she moved. And it made his blood beat violently. He ached for her to come nearer.

Dear God, she was right. Had some demon created her just to torment him, to make him lose the last shreds of his sanity?

It had been a week since he'd made love to her, a week since he'd found out her true identity. Seven days of ever-worsening hell.

"Damn you. Go home." But in his imagination he stripped her naked.

"No!" She took off her hat and with a defiant flick of her wrist flung it sailing down the circular stairwell.

When she walked toward him, he wanted to seize her, to pull her beneath his body. Instead he recoiled and stumbled blindly back into his bedroom. "If you're smart, you'll go."

"I have no choice, Joshua," she whispered in that shaking tone. "I'm playing for keeps."

So was he. He willed himself to be unmoved by her terror, by her seductive power, by his own fierce need to take her and punish her.

"You wanted revenge—well, take it. Take me. Use me. Destroy me. Get it all out of your system."

Never in all his life would he ever be able to get her out of his system. He tried to tear his eyes from the voluptuous curves of her lush body, from her soft mouth, but his pulse was beating abruptly in his throat. *She had offered herself to him.*

When she swayed closer, he caught the scent of jasmine and was intoxicated by more than liquor.

"Joshua, please..."

Something inside him broke, and he grabbed her and threw her down onto the bed. He fell on top of her, his massive body crushing hers. Her skin was like warm satin, her lips provocatively near, her breath warm and fragrant against his naked chest. A remnant of sanity in his whiskey-sodden mind warned him to let her go. But he didn't listen. She felt too good. She smelled too good. Other needs were all powerful.

He turned her face to his. "Do you know who you are? Why I have to hate you—"

"Does it matter?" she whispered, fighting to smile, her lips quivering instead.

His male reaction to her voluptous body mixed with the whiskey and his hatred, and the combination was as volatile as fire and gasoline. He felt hot and wild, wilder than he'd ever felt. Why did she have to feel so treacherously, dangerously good? Why did his pulse throb? Why couldn't he breathe? He wanted to hate her, to destroy her, but most of all he felt a volcanic rush of desire to make love to her.

"Your father killed my father! The Wyatt Hotel was my father's hotel. Hunter took it. And when he did, he took everything. My father felt like a failure after that. He started to drink. He abused me and my mother. He took risks. One day he was drinking and cleaning his gun. The gun went off and blew his brains out. Maybe it was suicide. That's something I'll never know." He paused for a long moment. His voice broke. "I—I found him. I was eleven. I blamed myself, because he'd gotten so mean I sometimes prayed he'd die."

"Oh, Joshua . . . I'm so sorry," she said gently, tenderly.

All his life he had craved gentleness, tenderness—love. Her pretense at those emotions and his craven need of them enraged him.

"Damn you. My father died because your father ruined him. My mother died, too. Hunter Wyatt put me in hell. Then you came along and finished the job."

She moaned softly. Fear and desire pooled in her wide eyes. "Because I didn't know—I'm sorry, Joshua. For what I did. For whatever my father did. The last thing I would ever want is to hurt you." She stroked his face very gently till he grabbed her hand and pulled it away. "But most of all I'm sorry for what you're doing to yourself."

"I don't believe you!" he yelled. "You're a liar! You don't give a damn about me!"

"No..."

But he couldn't bear to listen to more of her lies. When she tried to speak, his anger mushroomed like a spreading black haze. But so did his desire. He knew he shouldn't touch her; he knew he should throw her out before it was too late. But there was no way he could save himself. It was already too late.

Take or be taken. Use or be used. Destroy or be destroyed. She had done the same to him.

Her body lay beneath his. All he knew was that he could have her if he wanted her.

He ripped his jeans off. Then he stripped her, tearing buttons loose while she watched with big, frightened eyes.

When they were naked, he seized her hand and placed it on his thigh. "Touch me," he whispered. "You know the way I like it. Pretend again that you like it, too."

She flinched, wanting to draw back, but she didn't. Her hand went across iron muscle, circled him and moved with soft, sensual expertise until he groaned in an agony of savage pleasure. Tears slipped from her lashes and wet her cheeks.

Use or be used. He shoved her hand away and caught her in a powerful embrace and brought his mouth down to hers, his intention to ravage with bruising kisses, but when she kissed him, all the sweetness of her soul seemed to pour into his and become part of him. And it was as if he had entered a sensuous dream, and his fierce will was no longer his own but hers, too, and he could neither hurt nor destroy her. Some force that was stronger than his hatred made him gentle.

How could he hurt her when all he had ever wanted to do was love her? So he murmured velvet-tender love words as he gently kissed away her salty tears, which glistened like jewels upon her pale cheeks. He took his time until she was so eager she wrapped her legs around his waist and cried out for him to take her. He stroked her private satin flesh until she was ready and damp and clinging and arching her body into his, her need no longer sacrificial but a passion that burned with the same terrible, bright heat as his.

He made her wait, making love to her hungrily with his tongue, tasting her long and slowly until she shuddered with ecstacy against his mouth, until he drove himself mad. A long time later he drew her body beneath his and came inside her, at last, and again her body was like warm, writhing velvet. She was hot and tight and meltingly moist. And wild. Wilder and more wonderful than before. He knew that he would love her till he died.

When their crisis came together, they clung shuddering as if not only their bodies but their souls were joined.

Afterward, in the lengthening silence, they still held one another. It took a while before he fell back into himself, before he remembered her hateful identity. *Cecilia Wyatt!* How could he know her and still want her? She was the daughter of his father's killer. Her every word had been a lie. Her every kiss an act.

If he were a fool to still want her, he'd be much more of a fool to let her suspect how completely she had him in her power.

His frigid voice was low and harsh when he at last summoned the will to speak; his bitter eyes, blue ice. "Go home, *Cecilia.* You were good, but not good enough. I still intend to go after your father."

Her strangled cry tore his heart.

She was in his blood. He wanted the warmth of her skin next to his, the scent of her perfume every morning when he awoke.

He turned his back to her and lay still, feigning stony indifference as she got up, gathered her clothes and ran out.

After she was gone, the house was colder and lonelier than before. He was lonelier. He felt like a wounded beast whose heart had been torn out. The terrible silence almost drove him mad.

Then the phone rang, and his machine caught it.

The phone rang again.

And something told him to answer it.

A stranger's voice. A woman's.

What she said jolted him wide-awake like the most chilling scream of a nightmare.

His body turned to ice as her staccato words burst across his frantic brain.

"Terrible car wreck... His car rolled.... It took them more than an hour to cut him out. Marin County across the Golden Gate Bridge..."

Midnight was in the hospital intensive-care unit—dying.

And Joshua knew it was all his fault.

More than anything in all the world he needed Honey to help him face this nightmare. He hung up the phone and dialed her number, but when she heard his voice she made a low, almost inarticulate sound that contained all the loss and anguish in her soul.

The one broken word she spoke was his name. *"Joshua."*

Then the line went dead, and he felt as if her gentle voice had torn out his heart.

He remembered the last breathless, ravaging hour they'd spent together in his bed. The insidiously erotic power she held over him, his deep need for her and his fierce agony had nothing to do with hatred and everything to do with love.

He had been a proud, doomed fool not to forgive her, not to realize that he couldn't live without her.

But it was too late.

She was gone forever. He had driven her away just as he'd driven Midnight to his death.

Fourteen

"*You can't go in there!*"

The hell he couldn't. To hell with hospitals and all their stupid rules.

Joshua barged angrily through the shiny doors. Three gloved orderlies in masks and scrub suits rushed up to restrain him, but with deadly instincts honed in the gutter Joshua fought them off, slamming one against the wall and the others against a table, upsetting a tray of sterile instruments that clattered onto the tile floor.

That was the easy part. Then he saw Midnight lying gray faced and as still as death on a bloodstained stretcher beneath brilliant lights, and something inside Joshua shattered into a million pieces.

Doctors and nurses were speaking in hushed, urgent whispers, working frantically to prepare Midnight for surgery.

As Joshua slowly crossed the room, he realized he had never seen Midnight helpless before. His handsome features were slack. Black bruises circled his inky-lashed, shuttered eyes. His nose was broken and his mouth was cut and grotesquely puffy. There was a bloody patch on his forehead where the skin had been abraded by the steering wheel or the windshield.

A nurse was shaving his coal dark hair for brain surgery.

Joshua pressed Midnight's lifeless fingers and felt nauseated when he remembered that last time he'd touched his father's hand. What finished him off was the small plastic bag that a nurse stuffed into his hand.

A tremor went through him as he fumbled to open it.

Midnight's ring and watch.

Cold sweat broke out on Joshua's brow. The same clammy stuff ran down his back. His temples throbbed. Everything blurred. He felt as weak as a kitten, so weak he had to be helped back to the waiting room.

Hours passed, but Joshua had no concept of time; only of an ever darkening nightmare in which the horrors of his past mingled with the horrors of the present. It was his eleventh birthday and his first day at his terrible new school. A gang of street kids twice his size greeted him at the water fountain by slamming him against a graffiti-splattered locker and laughing at him because he was small and new and friendless and therefore defenseless. They made him the butt of their humiliating jokes, knocking the locker door into him at every punch line, shoving him mercilessly from one bully to another, until he felt even smaller, until he got dizzier and dizzier until he was so sick he threw up all over himself. That had made them laugh all the harder. Then Midnight was there, taller and tougher than any of them and meaner too—except for his eyes. The bullies had slunk away. And Midnight had been there ever since.

Till now.

Midnight had taught him to fight, had taught him to survive. Midnight had been the only one who understood his pain, and Midnight had always wanted him to get past it. It was a bitter irony that Midnight's last battle against the darkness in Joshua's soul was probably going to cost him his own life.

And Joshua knew he had never been worth it. He had always been a lost soul. The demons inside him had made him drive his only friend to his death. Just as they'd driven him to use Honey when she'd come to him to save her father; just as they'd driven him to cut her heart out with the roughest words he'd ever used on any woman.

Destroy or be destroyed.

He loved Midnight. And he loved Honey. His own daughter didn't want to live with him anymore. He loved her, too.

But the dark demons that were destroying him had made him destroy them all.

He would have given everything he had to die in Midnight's place.

Then Lacy was there in that tiny waiting room, and everything was worse because beside her was a skinny nine-year-old boy with coal-dark hair and coal-dark rebellious eyes. The kid had a distinctive strip of white in his hair that dripped low over his brow.

Lacy looked tired and scared, and Joshua remembered the dangerous man who was after her.

"You're supposed to be on that flight to Brazil."

"I couldn't go after I heard," Lacy said gently. "I—I couldn't leave Johnny... because... I just couldn't." She nudged the boy forward. "This is Joe," Lacy murmured.

Joshua looked into the boy's black eyes and missed a heartbeat.

Midnight, who loved children, had a son.

And because of Joshua, Midnight would probably die without ever knowing. Lacy and his child would be in terrible danger. If something happened to them because they had stayed in the States, their deaths would be Joshua's fault as well.

"It's too late to tell him," Joshua muttered. "He's unconscious and they don't think he'll ever wake up."

Joshua buried his head in his hands and let the black, numbing despair close around him.

And as he waited, even with Lacy there, without Honey, he felt alone during those long, dark hours, and more than anything he wished he could die instead of Midnight.

Pink light was pouring into the waiting room, but Joshua was scarcely aware of it. He felt stiff as he hunched forward, elbows on his jeans, his dark head collapsed in his hands. He twisted his wrist and looked wearily at his watch. Midnight had been in surgery more than five hours.

Dear God. The waiting was killing him. Then the bitter thought came: *If only it would.* Lacy had taken Joe downstairs to get something to eat.

A door was pushed open. Soft, tentative footsteps alerted him that he was no longer alone. God, the last thing he wanted was company. But he looked up, his dark face, haggard and angry and lost.

A woman was backlighted by the glow of the pink dawn light so that she looked like an angel with a shining aura. Her hair seemed on fire. Her face was in shadow.

But he knew who she was.

She moved toward him in vinyl boots, with earrings that jingled.

"Joshua—"

The soft tissue of his heart seemed to tear as her velvet voice shivered through him.

"Go away," he muttered fiercely. Even as he said that some part of him wanted to get down on his knees and beg her to stay.

He hunched lower, into himself, fighting to ignore her. But she just tiptoed defiantly closer and smiled *that* soft smile that he would always love.

Dear God, did she know what she was doing to him?

"Why the hell don't you ever obey me?" he growled, drawn, as always by her defiance, by her loveliness, but determined not to show it.

He shut his eyes and buried his head in his hands to resist the temptation of looking at her.

"How the hell did you know where I was?" he asked in a thick, anguished voice.

"Heather called."

"She shouldn't have bothered."

Honey took a faltering step toward him. "I'm sorry I hung up on you. I—I didn't know about Midnight."

Joshua kept his hands over his eyes, afraid of the sick, tense eagerness that made his stomach churn.

"How's Midnight?" she asked ever so gently.

"Not good," he managed. "He's still in surgery."

"He's tough."

"Even the toughest guys are human," he said unemotionally.

"I'm glad you finally learned that."

A great stillness descended on him. All he could hear was his heart slamming against his rib cage. "Look, I don't want you here."

"I know that."

He heard the sob in her voice as she took another step toward him. He held his breath, more afraid than he'd ever been.

The silence lengthened. He didn't know what else to say, what to do. Some unbearable tension began to build like an explosive force.

Then a door was thrown open and Midnight's surgeon, a beautiful woman with red hair and tense brown eyes, walked into the room.

"Who the hell—?" Joshua demanded, looking up. Then he saw how her brown eyes were circled with dark rings of exhaustion, and he shut up.

Dr. Lescuer nervously thumbed a two-inch-thick chart and set it down. "We nearly lost him—twice." She paused. "But after a while, things began to go better for us. We gave him blood. Got him stabilized. Then we removed bits of bone and metal from the thalamus and hippocampus fibrous regions of his brain. He was lucky as hell—a millimeter away from death or vital brain functions being destroyed. His leg and ribs and the surface cuts on his face were easy after that. If he makes it through the night, I'd say he's got at least a fifty-fifty chance. The surgery went off better than we expected. But..."

"But?"

"Even though we don't think there's been any permanent damage to the brain, he's been shaken up pretty badly."

"What do you mean?"

"There could be problems, disorientation for a while, maybe even some amnesia," the doctor said. "In a case like this, you can never predict the outcome. He could be moody, different."

Midnight would probably live. He had a fifty-fifty chance. That was all that mattered for now. And Lacy would be with him.

When the surgeon left, Joshua looked at Honey for the first time. Her face was pale, her green eyes huge and luminous, concerned.

Honey's gentle, reassuring smile cut out his heart. Dear God— Maybe Midnight would live, but he'd lost Honey.

Anguish made Joshua's features hard and set. His voice was harsh. "Thanks for coming."

For a moment her throat seemed so dry she couldn't speak. "I—I can't stay." She too looked anywhere but at him. "My father was furious when I told him where—"

Somehow Joshua kept his voice calm. "Don't stay on my account."

She went very still. "I knew you wouldn't want me here." Then she swallowed. "Goodbye, Joshua."

His heart slammed in slow, painful strokes as he watched her walk away.

She was at the door.

"Why did you have to come today?" he whispered.

"Oh, Joshua—"

Scalding tears slipped from her eyes and ran down her cheeks, and he saw how terribly he'd hurt her.

He heard her passionate whisper as if in a dream. "I'm sorry, Joshua. For what I did—for hurting you. For coming here when you don't want me. I hope I didn't make this worse. I understand why you hate me."

Her white face held the same wild pain that filled his soul. *Let her go.*

How could he? Then his life would be utter, soul-destroying desolation. He'd lived like that too long.

He got up slowly. "I don't hate you."

She swallowed a convulsive sob. "I—I just had to make sure you were okay." She pushed the door open. "Now that I know—"

He started running. "Hey, I'm not okay," he whispered fiercely, grabbing her arm in desperation. "I'll never be okay—not if you leave me." He pulled her back into the room, against his body.

"Joshua, what are you saying?"

"That I've been a crazy, stupid fool. Honey, I love you."

"I can't believe—"

"Believe it! I love you," he repeated in a low, tormented tone. "And I'm sorry, sorrier than you'll ever know—about a lot of things—for getting crazy drunk and hurting you the way my father used to hurt me. For quarreling with Midnight when he defended you, so that he drove so recklessly he damn near killed himself."

"Midnight and I were just as much at fault—"

"No— You both fought to save me." Joshua gave a deep sigh and drew her closer. "You are so beautiful...."

"But I'm not glamorous—"

He felt a terrible, growing constriction in his throat. "In my phony world, you're the only thing that's real."

"I'll never be skinny and glamorous enough to wear skintight sequins."

His eyes blazed with unspoken needs. "You look perfect—naked. Instead of sequins, I'll give you emeralds—to wear in bed."

"All I ever want is your love." She clung to him, her face shining.

He liked the way her length fit his, snugly, warmly, securely. His heart thundered. A white heat swept him. His hands smoothed her hair, touched her face reverently. "I never knew I could want anyone this much," he whispered fervently.

Her lashes were lowered. A soft cry of joy escaped her lips.

"I think I loved you from the first," he whispered. "Even when I knew who you were. You made the hate begin to go away. You brought me closer to Heather. I was very set on revenge, but your love and idealism lit a bright path out of the darkness. Oh, Honey, there were so many years of darkness."

Their gazes melted together. She brushed her fingertips across his lips. "I couldn't bear the thought of losing you either," she admitted very softly. "That's why I came today. Because I had to see you. I was so afraid you'd blame yourself—"

"But your father—" he whispered.

"Oh, Joshua, I don't care if he ever forgives me. Astella is on my side now, and she'll try to win him over. But I love you too much to give you up—for anybody." Honey kept smoothing his hair gently with her trembling hands. "I wanted his approval and I could never have it. So I married Mike and pretended that I was good and morally superior like him and that what I really wanted was to save the world. Now...at last, for the first time, I feel like I'm beginning to know who I am and what I really want and I don't care if anybody approves. Because I know you are right for me. And this new belief in myself is something wonderful that grew out of my feelings for you. You weren't what I thought I wanted, but I love you anyway. I love you so much that everything, even my family...even wanting to find my brother, Raven, pales in significance. Mario will be better off. He needs a father."

"And Heather and I need you," Joshua said, kissing her, softly at first, and then with an intensity that left no doubt about the depth of his feelings. "I don't deserve you. I'll never be good enough for you."

When he kissed Honey again, wildfire pulsed in his blood. And as his searing mouth stole the very breath from her lips, he surrendered his soul to the only woman he had ever loved. She smelled sweet and wondrous. She was his. Only his.

They held each other, shuddering with delight as they kissed and nuzzled while the heat of their love and the fire of a new sun enveloped them in glorious flooding warmth.

There had never been a hotter or a wilder dawn.

Epilogue

Raven's gift arrived a month after Honey's wedding, three months after Midnight's accident, the first Saturday they got back from their honeymoon in Hawaii. It was huge and wrapped in shiny psychedelic *green* paper, her favorite shade of green. There was no return address, nothing but his first name written in a slanting, bold hand on the outside and the drawing of a tiny raven beneath the name. The mysterious gift was delivered by a special courier who would say nothing about the sender.

Honey began to shake the minute she saw her brother's name and the familiar line drawing. How had he known she'd married? Where she lived? Why hadn't he come himself?

She was dying to open his gift, and yet it was too precious to open without Joshua and their family and friends at her side. So, she carried it up to the terrace where everything was set up to honor Midnight, who was now living on his houseboat with Lacy and Joe.

The package was such a hot, brilliant green that she couldn't take her eyes off it. She could hardly wait to open it, but she waited. Only when Midnight walked slowly out of the elevator and onto the terrace with Lacy and everyone had laughed that so much green and so much clutter had crept into Joshua's home in just four weeks, only after the champagne corks had been popped and glasses filled, did she unwrap her present and gasp with pleasure when she discovered a long lost painting her mother had done of her and Raven.

Tears sprang in Honey's eyes as she looked at it, and she clung to Joshua. "It was the last thing Mother painted before she died. Raven knew how much I loved it," she whispered. "He loved it, too. That day was our last happy time together. I always wondered what happened to it."

"I like the way you wore your hair," Heather said, studying the picture.

"You were cute," Mario said. "But you had mischievous eyes."

"I was a brat," Honey replied.

Honey began to tear through the paper her brother's gift had come in. "H-he didn't send a note. Why—"

Joshua was silent.

"But at least I know he's still alive," Honey said. "Maybe some day soon he'll decide to come home. Until he does, I have you and Mario and Heather."

Midnight came closer and lifted his champagne glass to them. "To you, J.K., and to you, Honey, for finally doing what I'd been trying to do for years."

"And what the hell was that?" Joshua demanded.

"She saved your soul." Midnight's voice lowered, but he held his glass higher. "To your lasting happiness."

Joshua lifted his glass. "And to you, Midnight. You'll never know how I prayed for this day. To see you walk through my front door again, and with Lacy and Joe."

Midnight's expression darkened as he stared across the crowded terrace at Lacy, who seemed to be ignoring him. "Thanks. But they're not completely mine yet, J.K."

"Why not?" Joshua demanded.

"It's a long story. A lot happened while you two were away on your honeymoon. Last night Cole Douglas broke into my houseboat and scared the hell out of Lacy. He's in custody and I'm expecting a call from the lieutenant in charge of his case. We may have some answers soon about a lot of stuff that'll affect Lacy and me—I want her back, J.K." Midnight's expression was hard.

"Then what's stopping you?" Joshua asked.

"I'm not sure. A feeling in my gut. My brain's not working quite as good as it used to—"

"Good. Then maybe I can keep up with you."

Midnight set his champagne glass down with a tense smile. "I can tell from now on my life's going to be a living hell. Hey, I'd better look for Joe and let you two enjoy each other."

"Good luck, Midnight," Joshua said.

"He looks wonderful. He's going to be okay," Honey said reassuringly.

Joshua pulled her close and her nearness made him feel warm and loved. "I want Lacy and Midnight to find each other—the way we found each other."

"They will," Honey whispered.

But when the police called a few minutes later and Midnight dropped the phone and seized Lacy, dragging her away with a dark, shattered look on his face, Honey saw that Joshua was very worried.

Not that he mentioned his friend until hours later when their guests had gone and Honey and Joshua were alone in their bedroom getting ready for bed.

Joshua ripped off his cuff links. "Did you notice how upset Midnight looked with Lacy when he ran out? I thought things might work out between them until he did that."

Honey took off her emerald earrings. "Trust me. He loves her. He never took his eyes off her."

"But why did he run off like that looking like he hated her?"

"I seem to remember you looking at me once or twice like
that," she said with a smile. "They're going to find each
other—the way we found each other."

Suddenly he knew she was right. "When two people really love each other," he said huskily, "they find a way to
work out their problems."

She laughed. "I can't believe this! You're beginning to
sound like an incurable romantic."

Joshua opened a window and got into bed. "Hey, you
were the one who taught me to believe in the power of love
to work miracles. Lacy has come back to Midnight. They've
both been through hell, but he'll accept her back completely in his life—he just needs time." Joshua turned out
the light and the room melted into starry darkness. Cool
night air that was scented from the flowers blooming in the
garden drifted into the bedroom. "Come here," he said
huskily.

"I was trying to have a serious conversation."

"I want to give you a hands-on lesson about the power of
love. We'll worry about Midnight tomorrow." He took the
phone off the hook and buried it under a pillow.

She got into bed wearing only her sparkling emerald ring.
Her naked body slid into Joshua's warmth. Midnight and
Lacy would have to work out their own problems the way
she and Joshua had. And Joshua was right—the greatest
power on earth was love.

Joshua's arms wound around her. His mouth found hers
in the darkness. Her soft body nestled against his hard,
muscular length. As always his skin was incredibly hot, his
kisses stirring her to incredible heights. And what happened was something wild, something so shattering that it
involved all her senses as well as her soul. And when it was
over, it wasn't over at all because she lay in his arms the rest
of the night, satiated and yet basking in the incredible security of his love, which she knew would last as long as they
lived and forever.

*   *   *   *   *

Silhouette Books has done it again!

Opening night in October has never been as exciting! Come watch as the curtain rises and romance flourishes when the stars of tomorrow make their debuts today!

Revel in Jodi O'Donnell's STILL SWEET ON HIM—
Silhouette Romance #969
...as Callie Farrell's renovation of the family homestead leads her straight into the arms of teenage crush Drew Barnett!

Tingle with Carol Devine's BEAUTY AND THE BEASTMASTER—
Silhouette Desire #816
...as legal eagle Amanda Tarkington is carried off by wrestler Bram Masterson!

Thrill to Elyn Day's A BED OF ROSES—
Silhouette Special Edition #846
...as Dana Whitaker's body and soul are healed by sexy physical therapist Michael Gordon!

Believe when Kylie Brant's McLAIN'S LAW —
Silhouette Intimate Moments #528
...takes you into detective Connor McLain's life as he falls for psychic—and suspect—Michele Easton!

Catch the classics of tomorrow—*premiering* today—
only from V. Silhouette

WOLFE WAITING
by Joan Hohl

This big, bad Wolfe never had to huff and puff and blow down *any* woman's door—scrumptiously sexy rookie officer Jake Wolfe was just too tempting and tasty to leave outside in the cold! But then he got hungry for answers from the suspicious lady who wouldn't let him two feet near her. What was a big, bad Wolfe to do?
